DESCRIPTION OF A STRUGGLE

Franz Kafka

DESCRIPTION
OF A STRUGGLE

SCHOCKEN BOOKS NEW YORK

TRANSLATED BY

TANIA AND JAMES STERN

Publisher's Note

The stories in this volume are presented
for the first time in English.
The original German text is contained
in *Beschreibung eines Kampfes.*

The title story, which Kafka wrote at the
age of twenty, is the only complete
piece from his early period.
For a long time considered lost,
it turned up in Max Brod's library,
together with the fragment of the novel,
Wedding Preparations in the Country.

The Warden of the Tomb is the
novelist's only piece in drama form;
it was contained in one of
Kafka's blue octavo notebooks and,
partly, in a typescript.

CONTENTS

DESCRIPTION
OF A STRUGGLE

And people in their Sunday best
Stroll about, swaying over the gravel
Under this enormous sky
Which, from hills in the distance,
Stretches to distant hills.

I

At about midnight a few people rose, bowed, shook hands, said it had been a pleasant evening, and then passed through the wide doorway into the vestibule, to put on their coats. The hostess stood in the middle of the room and made graceful bowing movements, causing the dainty folds in her skirt to move up and down.

I sat at a tiny table—it had three curved, thin legs—sipping my third glass of benedictine, and while I drank I surveyed my little store of pastry which I myself had picked out and arranged in a pile.

Then I saw my new acquaintance, somewhat dishevelled and out of shape, appear at the doorpost of an adjoining room; but I tried to look away for it was no concern of mine. He, however, came toward me and, smiling absent-mindedly at my occupation, said: "Excuse me for disturbing you, but until this very moment I've been sitting alone with my girl in the room next door. Ever since half-past ten. Lord, what an evening! I know it isn't right for me to be telling you this, for we hardly know one another. We only met on the stairs this evening and exchanged a few words as guests of the same house. And now—but you must forgive me, please—my happiness just cannot be contained, I can't help it. And since I have no other acquaintance here whom I can trust ——"

I looked at him sadly—the piece of fruitcake which I had in my mouth did not taste particularly good—and said into his rather flushed face: "I'm glad of course that you consider me trustworthy, but displeased that you have confided in me. And you yourself, if you weren't in such a state, would know how improper it is to talk about an amorous girl to a man sitting alone drinking schnapps."

When I said this he sat down with a jolt, leaned back in his chair, and let his arms hang down. Then he pressed them back, his elbows pointed, and began talking in rather a loud voice: "Only a little while ago we were alone in that room, Annie and I. And I kissed her, I kissed her—her mouth, her ears, her shoulders. Oh, my Lord and Saviour!"

A few guests, suspecting ours to be a rather more animated conversation, approached us closer, yawning. Whereupon I stood up and said so that all could hear: "All right then, if you insist, I'll go with you, but I repeat: it's ridiculous to climb up the Laurenziberg now, in winter and in the middle of the night. Besides, it's freezing, and as it has been snowing the roads out there are like skating rinks. Well, as you like——"

At first he gazed at me in astonishment and parted his wet lips; but then, noticing the guests who had approached quite close, he laughed, stood up, and said: "I think the cold will do us good; our clothes are full of heat and smoke; what's more, I'm slightly tipsy without having drunk very much; yes, let's say good-by and go."

So we went to the hostess, and as he kissed

13

her hand she said: "I am glad to see you looking so happy today."

Touched by the kindness of these words, he
kissed her hand again; whereupon she smiled.
I had to drag him away. In the vestibule stood
a housemaid, whom we hadn't seen before. She
helped us into our coats and then took a small
lantern to light us down the stairs. Her neck
was bare save for a black velvet ribbon round
her throat; her loosely clothed body was
stooped and kept stretching as she went down
the stairs before us, holding the lantern low.
Her cheeks were flushed, for she had drunk
some wine, and in the weak lamplight which
filled the whole stairwell, I could see her lips
trembling.

At the foot of the stairs she put down the
lantern, took a step towards my acquaintance,
embraced him, kissed him, and remained in
the embrace. Only when I pressed a coin into
her hand did she drowsily detach her arms
from him, slowly open the front door, and let
us out into the night.

Over the deserted, evenly lit street stood a

large moon in a slightly clouded, and therefore unusually extended, sky. On the frozen snow one had to take short steps.

Hardly were we outside when I evidently began to feel very gay. I raised my legs, let my joints crack, I shouted a name down the street as though a friend of mine had just vanished round the corner; leaping, I threw my hat in the air and caught it boastfully.

My acquaintance, however, walked on beside me, unconcerned. He held his head bent. He didn't even speak.

This surprised me, for I had calculated that he, once I had got him away from the party, would give vent to his joy. Now I too could calm down. No sooner had I given him an encouraging slap on the back than I suddenly no longer understood his mood, and withdrew my hand. Since I had no use for it, I stuck it in the pocket of my coat.

So we walked on in silence. Listening to the sound of our steps, I couldn't understand why I was incapable of keeping step with my acquaintance—especially since the air was clear and I could see his legs quite plainly. Here and there someone leaned out of a window and watched us.

On turning into the Ferdinandstrasse I realized that my acquaintance had begun to hum a melody from the *Dollar Princess*. It was low, but I could hear it distinctly. What did this mean? Was he trying to insult me? As for me, I was ready to do without not only this music, but the walk as well. Why wasn't he speaking to me, anyway? And if he didn't need me, why hadn't he left me in peace in the warm room with the benedictine and the pastry? It certainly wasn't I who had insisted on this walk. Besides, I could have gone for a walk on my own. I had merely been at a party, had saved an ungrateful young man from disgrace, and was now wandering about in the moonlight. That was all right, too. All day in the office, evenings at a party, at night in the streets, and nothing to excess. A way of life so natural that it borders on the excessive!

Yet my acquaintance was still behind me. Indeed, he even quickened his steps when he realized that he had fallen in the rear. No word was uttered, nor could it be said that we were running. But I wondered if it wouldn't be a good idea to turn down a side street; after all, I wasn't obliged to go on this walk with him. I could go home alone and no one could stop me. Then, secretly, I could watch my acquaintance pass the entrance to my street. Good-by, dear acquaintance! On reaching my room I'll feel warm, I'll light the lamp in its iron stand on my table, and when I've done that I'll lie back in my armchair which stands on the torn Oriental carpet. Pleasant prospects! Why not? But then? No then. The lamp will shine in the warm room, shine on my chest as I lie in the armchair. Then I'll cool off and spend hours alone between the painted walls and the floor which, reflected in the gilt-framed mirror hanging on the rear wall, appears slanted.

My legs were growing tired and I had already decided to go home and lie down, when I began to wonder if, before going away, I ought to say good night to my acquaintance. But I was too timid to go away without a word and too weak to call to him out loud. So I stood still, leaned against the moonlit wall of a house, and waited.

My acquaintance came sailing along the pavement toward me as fast as though he expected me to catch him. He winked at me, suggesting some agreement which I had apparently forgotten.

"What's up?" I asked.

"Oh, nothing," he said. "I only wanted to ask your opinion about that housemaid who kissed me on the staircase. Who is the girl? Have you ever seen her before? No? Nor have I. Was she a housemaid at all? I had meant to ask you this before, while she was walking down the stairs in front of us."

"I saw at once by her red hands that she's a housemaid, and not even the first housemaid, and when I gave her the money I felt her hard skin."

"But that merely proves that she has been some time in service, which no doubt is the case."

"You may be right about that. In that light one couldn't distinguish everything, but her face reminded me of the elder daughter of an officer I happen to know."

"Not me," he said.

"That won't stop me going home; it's late and I have to be in the office early. One sleeps badly there." Whereupon I put out my hand to say good-by to him.

"Whew, what a cold hand!" he cried. "I wouldn't like to go home with a hand like that. You should have let yourself be kissed, too, my friend. That was an omission. Still, you can make up for it. But sleep? On a night like this? What an idea! Just think how many thoughts a blanket smothers while one lies alone in bed, and how many unhappy dreams it keeps warm."

"I neither smother anything nor warm anything," I said.

"Oh, go on!" he concluded, "you're a humorist!"

At the same time he began walking again and I followed without realizing it, for I was busy thinking of what he had said.

From these words I imagined that my acquaintance suspected in me something which, although it wasn't there, made me nevertheless rise in his estimation by his suspecting it. So it was just as well I hadn't gone home. Who knows, this man—thinking of housemaid affairs while walking beside me, his mouth steaming with cold—might be capable of bestowing on me in the eyes of the world a value without my having to work for it. Let's pray the girls won't spoil him! By all means let them kiss and hug him, that's their duty and his right, but they mustn't carry him off. After all, when they kiss him they also kiss me a little— with the corners of their mouths, so to speak. But if they carry him off, then they steal him from me. And he must always remain with me, always. Who is to protect him, if not I? And he's so stupid. Someone says to him in February: Come up the Laurenziberg—and off he goes. And supposing he falls down now, or catches cold? Suppose some jealous man appears from the Postgasse and attacks him? What will happen to me? Am I to be just kicked out of the world? I'll believe that when I see it! No, he won't get rid of me.

Tomorrow he'll be talking to Fräulein Anna, about ordinary things at first, as is natural, but suddenly he won't be able to keep it from her any longer: Last night, Annie, after the party, you remember, I was with a man the like of whom you've certainly never seen. He looked—how can I describe him to you?—like a stick dangling in the air, he looked, with a black-haired skull on top. His body was clad in a lot of small dull-yellow patches of cloth which covered him completely because they hung closely about him in the still air of last night. Well, Annie, does that spoil your appetite? It does? In that case it's my fault, then I told the whole thing badly. If only you'd seen him, walking timidly beside me, reading infatuation on my face (which wasn't very difficult) and going a long way ahead of me so as not to disturb me. I think, Annie, you'd have laughed a bit and been a bit afraid; but I was glad of his company. For where were you, Annie? You were in your bed, and your bed was far away—it might just as well have been in Africa. But sometimes I really felt as though the starry sky rose and fell with the gasping of his flat chest. You think I'm exaggerating? No, Annie. Upon my soul, no. Upon my soul which belongs to you, no.

And I didn't spare my acquaintance—we had just reached the first steps of the Franzensquai—the smallest fraction of the humiliation he must have felt at making such a speech. Save that my thoughts grew blurred at this moment, for the Moldau and the quarter of the town on the farther shore lay together in the dark. A number of lights burning there teased the eye.

We crossed the road in order to reach the railing along the river, and there we stood still. I found a tree to lean against. Because of the cold blowing up from the water, I put on my gloves, sighed for no good reason as one is inclined to do at night beside a river, but then I wanted to walk on. My acquaintance, however, was staring into the water, and didn't budge. Then he moved closer to the railing; his legs were already against the iron bar, he propped his elbows up and laid his forehead in his hands. What next? After all, I was shivering and had to put up the collar of my coat.

My acquaintance stretched himself—his back, shoulders, neck—and held the upper half of his body, which rested on his taut arms, bent over the railing.

"Oh well, memories," said I. "Yes, even re-membering in itself is sad, yet how much more its object! Don't let yourself in for things like that, it's not for you and not for me. It only weakens one's present position without strengthening the former one—nothing is more obvious—quite apart from the fact that the former one doesn't need strengthening. Do you think I have no memories? Oh, ten for every one of yours. Now, for instance, I could remember sitting on a bench in L. It was in the evening, also near a river. In summer, of course. And on such evenings it's my habit to pull up my legs and put my arms round them. I had leaned my head against the wooden back of the bench, and from there I watched the cloudlike mountains on the other shore. A violin was playing softly in the hotel by the river. Now and again on both shores trains chuffed by amidst shining smoke."

Turning suddenly round, my acquaintance

interrupted me; he almost looked as though he were surprised to see me still here. "Oh, I could tell you much more," I said, nothing else.

"Just imagine," he began, "and it always happens like this. Today, as I was going downstairs to take a short walk before the evening party, I couldn't help being surprised by the way my hands were dangling about in my cuffs, and they were doing it so gaily. Which promptly made me think: Just wait, something's going to happen today. And it did, too." He said this while turning to go and looked at me smiling out of his big eyes.

So I had already got as far as that. He could tell me things like that and at the same time smile and look at me with big eyes. And I—I had to restrain myself from putting my arm round his shoulders and kissing him on the eyes as a reward for having absolutely no use for me. But the worst was that even that could no longer do any harm because it couldn't change anything, for now I had to go away, away at any price.

While I was still trying urgently to think

of some means by which I could stay at least a little while longer with my acquaintance, it occurred to me that perhaps my long body displeased him by making him feel too small. And this thought—although it was late at night and we had hardly met a soul—tormented me so much that while walking I bent my back until my hands reached my knees. But in order to prevent my acquaintance from noticing my intentions I changed my position only very gradually, tried to divert his attention from myself, once even turning him towards the river, pointing out to him with outstretched hands the trees on the Schützeninsel and the way the bridge lamps were reflected in the river.

But wheeling suddenly round, he looked at me—I hadn't quite finished yet—and said: "What's this? You're all crooked! What on earth are you up to?"

"Quite right. You're very observant," said I, my head on the seam of his trousers, which was why I couldn't look up properly.

"Enough of that! Stand up straight! What nonsense!"

"No," I said, my face close to the ground, "I'll stay as I am."

"You really can annoy a person, I must say. Such a waste of time! Come on, put an end to it."

"The way you shout! In the quiet of the night!" I said.

"Oh well, just as you like," he added, and after a while: "It's a quarter to one." He had evidently seen the time on the clock of the Mühlenturm.

I promptly stood up straight as though I'd been pulled up by the hair. For a while I kept my mouth open, to let my agitation escape. I understood: he was sending me away. There was no place for me near him, or if there were one, at least it could not be found. Why, by the way, was I so intent on staying with him? No, I ought to go away—and this at once—to my relatives and friends who were waiting for me. But if I didn't have any relatives and friends then I must fend for myself (what was the good of complaining!), but I must leave here no less quickly. For in his eyes nothing could redeem me any longer, neither my length, my appetite, nor my cold hand. But if I were of the opinion that I had to remain with him, it was a dangerous opinion.

"I wasn't in need of your information," I said, which happened to be true.

"Thank God you're standing up straight again. All I said was that it's a quarter to one."

"That's all right," said I, and stuck two fingernails in the gaps between my chattering teeth. "If I didn't need your information, how much less do I need an explanation. The fact is, I need nothing but your mercy. Please, take back what you said just now!"

"That it's a quarter to one? But with pleasure, especially since a quarter to one passed long ago."

He lifted his right arm, flicked his hand, and listened to the castanetlike sound of his cuff links.

Obviously, this is the time for the murder. I'll stay with him and slowly he'll draw the dagger—the handle of which he is already holding in his pocket—along his coat, and then plunge it into me. It's unlikely that he'll be surprised at the simplicity of it all—yet

27

maybe he will, who knows? I won't scream, I'll just stare at him as long as my eyes can stand it.

"Well?" he said.

In front of a distant coffeehouse with black windowpanes a policeman let himself glide over the pavement like a skater. His sword hampering him, he took it in his hand, and now he glided along for quite a while, finally ending up by almost describing a circle. At last he yodelled weakly and, melodies in his head, began once more to skate.

It wasn't until the arrival of this policeman —who, two hundred feet from an imminent murder, saw and heard only himself—that I began to feel a certain fear. I realized that whether I allowed myself to be stabbed or ran away, my end had come. Would it not be better, then, to run away and thus expose myself to a difficult and therefore more painful death? I could not immediately put my finger on the reasons in favor of this form of death, but I couldn't afford to spend my last remaining seconds looking for reasons. There would be time for that later provided I had the determination, and the determination I had.

I had to run away, it would be quite easy. At the turning to the left onto the Karlsbrücke I could jump to the right into the Karlsgasse. It was winding, there were dark doorways, and taverns still open; I didn't need to despair.

As we stepped from under the arch at the end of the quay onto the Kreuzherrenplatz, I ran into that street with my arms raised. But in front of a small door in the Seminarkirche I fell, for there was a step which I had not expected. It made a little noise, the next street lamp was sufficiently far away, I lay in the dark.

From a tavern opposite came a fat woman with a lantern to see what had happened in the street. The piano within continued playing, but fainter, with only one hand, because the pianist had turned towards the door which, until now ajar, had been opened wide by a man in a high-buttoned coat. He spat and then hugged the woman so hard she was obliged to raise the lantern in order to protect it.

"Nothing's happened!" he shouted into the room, whereupon they both turned, went inside, and the door was closed.

When I tried to get up I fell down again. "Sheer ice," I said, and felt a pain in my knee. Yet I was glad that the people in the tavern hadn't seen me and that I could go on lying here peacefully until dawn.

My acquaintance had apparently walked on as far as the bridge without having noticed my disappearance, for it was some time before he joined me. I saw no signs of surprise as he bent down over me—lowering little more than his neck, exactly like a hyena—and stroked me with a soft hand. He passed it up and down my cheekbone and then laid his palm on my forehead. "You've hurt yourself, eh? Well, it's icy and one must be careful—didn't you tell me so yourself? Does your head ache? No? Oh, the knee. H'm. That's bad."

But it didn't occur to him to help me up. I supported my head with my right hand, my elbow on a cobblestone, and said: "Here we are together again." And as my fear was beginning to return, I pressed both hands against

his shinbone in order to push him away. "Do
go away," I said.

He had his hands in his pockets and looked
up the empty street, then at the Seminarkirche, then up at the sky. At last, at the sound
of a carriage in one of the near-by streets, he
remembered me: "Why don't you say something, my friend? Do you feel sick? Why don't
you get up? Shall I look for a cab? If you like,
I'll get you some wine from the tavern. In any
case, you mustn't lie here in the cold. Besides,
we wanted to go up the Laurenziberg."

"Of course," said I, and got up on my own,
but with great pain. I began to sway, and had
to look severely at the statue of Karl IV to be
sure of my position. However, even this would
not have helped me had I not remembered that
I was loved by a girl with a black velvet ribbon round her neck, if not passionately, at
least faithfully. And it really was kind of the
moon to shine on me, too, and out of modesty
I was about to place myself under the arch of
the tower bridge when it occurred to me that
the moon, of course, shone on everything. So
I happily spread out my arms in order fully

31

to enjoy the moon. And by making swimming movements with my weary arms it was easy for me to advance without pain or difficulty. To think that I had never tried this before! My head lay in the cool air and it was my right knee that flew best; I praised it by patting it. And I remembered that once upon a time I didn't altogether like an acquaintance, who was probably still walking below me, and the only thing that pleased me about the whole business was that my memory was good enough to remember even a thing like that. But I couldn't afford to do much thinking, for I had to go on swimming to prevent myself from sinking too low. However, to avoid being told later that anyone could swim on the pavement and that it wasn't worth mentioning, I raised myself above the railing by increasing my speed and swam in circles round the statue of every saint I encountered. At the fifth—I was holding myself just above the footpath by imperceptible flappings—my acquaintance gripped my hand. There I stood once more on the pavement and felt a pain in my knee.

"I've always admired," said my acquaintance, clutching me with one hand and pointing with the other at the statue of St. Ludmila, "I've always admired the hands of this angel here to the left. Just see how delicate they are! Real angel's hands! Have you ever seen anything like them? You haven't, but I have, for this evening I kissed hands——"

But for me there was now a third possibility of perishing. I didn't have to let myself be stabbed, I didn't have to run away, I could simply throw myself into the air. Let him go up his Laurenziberg, I won't interfere with him, not even by running away will I interfere with him.

And now I shouted: "Out with your stories! I no longer want to hear scraps. Tell me everything, from beginning to end. I won't listen to less, I warn you. But I'm burning to hear the whole thing." When he looked at me I stopped shouting so loud. "And you can count on my discretion! Tell me everything that's on your mind. You've never had so discreet a listener as I."

And rather low, close to his ear, I said: "And you don't need to be afraid of me, that's quite unnecessary."

I heard him laugh.

"Yes, yes," I said. "I believe that. I don't doubt it," and so saying I pinched him in the calves—where they were exposed. But he didn't feel it. Whereupon I said to myself: "Why walk with this man? You don't love him, nor do you hate him, because all he cares about is a girl and it's not even certain that she wears a white dress. So to you this man is indifferent —I repeat: indifferent. But he is also harmless, as has been proved. So walk on with him up the Laurenziberg, for you are already on your way, it's a beautiful night, but let him do the talking and enjoy yourself after your fashion, for this is the very best way (say it in a whisper) to protect yourself."

II

DIVERSIONS *or* PROOF THAT IT'S IMPOSSIBLE TO LIVE

i *A RIDE*

And now—with a flourish, as though it were not the first time—I leapt onto the shoulders of my acquaintance, and by digging my fists into his back I urged him into a trot. But since he stumped forward rather reluctantly and sometimes even stopped, I kicked him in the belly several times with my boots, to make him more lively. It worked and we came fast enough into the interior of a vast but as yet unfinished landscape.

The road on which I was riding was stony and rose considerably, but just this I liked and I let it become still stonier and steeper. As soon as my acquaintance stumbled I pulled him up by the collar and the moment he sighed I boxed his head. In doing so I felt how healthy this ride in the good air was for me, and in order to make him wilder I let a strong wind blow against us in long gusts.

Now I even began to exaggerate my jumping movements on my acquaintance's broad shoulders, and gripping his neck tight with both hands I bent my head far back and contemplated the many and various clouds which, weaker than I, sailed clumsily with the wind. I laughed and trembled with courage. My coat spread out and gave me strength. I pressed my hands hard together and in doing so happened to make my acquaintance choke. Only when the sky became gradually hidden by the branches of the trees, which I let grow along the road, did I come to myself.

"I don't know," I cried without a sound, "I really don't know. If nobody comes, then nobody comes. I have done nobody any harm, nobody has done me any harm, but nobody will help me. A pack of nobodies. But it isn't quite like that. It's just that nobody helps me, otherwise a pack of nobodies would be nice, I would rather like (what do you think?) to go on an excursion with a pack of nobodies. Into the mountains, of course, where else? Just look at these nobodies pushing each other, all these arms stretched across or hooked into one another, these feet separated by tiny steps! Everyone in frock coats, needless to say. We walk along so happily, a fine wind is whistling through the gaps made by us and our limbs. In the mountains our throats become free. It's a wonder we don't break into song."

Then my acquaintance collapsed, and when I examined him I discovered that he was badly wounded in the knee. Since he could no longer be of any use to me, I left him there on the stones without much regret and whistled down a few vultures which, obediently and with serious beaks, settled down on him in order to guard him.

ii *A WALK*

I walked on, unperturbed. But since, as a pedestrian, I dreaded the effort of climbing the mountainous road, I let it become gradually flatter, let it slope down into a valley in the distance. The stones vanished at my will and the wind disappeared.

I walked at a brisk pace and since I was on my way down I raised my head, stiffened my body, and crossed my arms behind my head. Because I love pinewoods I went through woods of this kind, and since I like gazing silently up at the stars, the stars appeared slowly in the sky, as is their wont. I saw only a few fleecy clouds which a wind, blowing just at their height, pulled through the air, to the astonishment of the pedestrian.

Opposite and at some distance from my road, probably separated from it by a river as well, I caused to rise an enormously high mountain whose plateau, overgrown with brushwood, bordered on the sky. I could see quite clearly the little ramifications of the highest branches and their movements. This sight, ordinary as it may be, made me so happy that I, as a small bird on a twig of those distant scrubby bushes, forgot to let the moon come up. It lay already behind the mountain, no doubt angry at the delay.

But now the cool light which precedes the rising of the moon spread over the mountain and suddenly the moon itself appeared from beyond one of the restless bushes. I on the other hand had meanwhile been gazing in another direction, and when I now looked ahead of me and suddenly saw it glowing in its almost full roundness, I stood still with troubled eyes, for my precipitous road seemed to lead straight into this terrifying moon.

After a while, however, I grew accustomed to it and watched with composure the difficulty it had in rising, until finally, having approached one another a considerable part of the way, I felt overcome by an intense drowsiness caused, I assumed, by the fatigue of the walk to which I was unaccustomed. I wandered on for a while with closed eyes, keeping myself awake only by a loud and regular clapping of my hands.

But then, as the road threatened to slip away from under my feet and everything, as weary as I myself, began to vanish, I summoned my remaining strength and hastened to scale the slope to the right of the road in order to reach in time the high tangled pinewood where I planned to spend the night that probably lay ahead of us.

The haste was necessary. The stars were already fading and I noticed the moon sink feebly into the sky as though into troubled waters. The mountain already belonged to the darkness, the road crumbled away at the point where I had turned towards the slope, and from the interior of the forest I heard the approaching crashes of collapsing trees. Now I could have thrown myself down on the moss to sleep, but since I feared to sleep on the ground I crept—the trunk sliding quickly down the rings formed by my arms and legs—up a tree which was already reeling without wind. I lay down on a branch and, leaning my head against the trunk, went hastily to sleep while a squirrel of my whim sat stiff-tailed at the trembling end of the branch, and rocked itself.

My sleep was deep and dreamless. Neither the waning moon nor the rising sun awoke me. And even when I was about to wake up, I calmed myself by saying: "You made a great effort yesterday, so spare your sleep," and went to sleep again.

Although I did not dream, my sleep was not free from a continuous slight disturbance. All night long I heard someone talking beside me.

The words themselves I could hardly hear—except isolated ones like "bench . . . by the river," "cloudlike mountains," "trains . . . amidst shining smoke"; what I did hear was the special kind of emphasis placed on them; and I remember that even in my sleep I rubbed my hands with pleasure at not being obliged to recognize single words, since I was asleep.

"Your life was monotonous," I said aloud in order to convince myself, "it really was necessary for you to be taken somewhere else. You ought to be content, it's gay here. The sun's shining."

Whereupon the sun shone and the rain clouds grew white and light and small in the blue sky. They sparkled and billowed out. I saw a river in the valley.

"Yes, your life was monotonous, you deserve this diversion," I continued as though compelled, "but was it not also perilous?" At that moment I heard someone sigh terribly near.

I tried to climb down quickly, but since the branch trembled as much as my hand I fell rigid from the top. I did not fall heavily, nor did I feel any pain, but I felt so weak and unhappy that I buried my face in the ground: I could not bear the strain of seeing around me the things of the earth. I felt convinced that every movement and every thought was forced, and that one had to be on one's guard against them. Yet nothing seemed more natural than to lie here on the grass, my arms beside my body, my face hidden. And I tried to persuade myself that I ought to be pleased to be already in this natural position, for otherwise many painful contortions, such as steps or words, would be required to arrive at it.

The river was wide and its noisy little waves reflected the light. On the other shore lay meadows which farther on merged into bushes behind which, at a great distance, one could see bright avenues of fruit trees leading to green hills.

Pleased by this sight, I lay down and, stopping my ears against the dread sound of sobs, I thought: Here I could be content. For here it is secluded and beautiful. It won't take much courage to live here. One will have to struggle here as anywhere else, but at least one won't have to do it with graceful movements. That

won't be necessary. For there are only mountains and a wide river and I have sense enough
to regard them as inanimate. Yes, when I totter
alone up the steep path through the meadows
in the evening I will be no more forsaken than
the mountains, except that I will feel it. But I
think that this, too, will pass.

Thus I toyed with my future life and tried
stubbornly to forget. And all the time I blinked
at that sky which was of an unusually promis-
ing color. It was a long time since I'd seen it
like this; I was moved and reminded of certain
days when I thought I had seen it in the same
way. I took my hands from my ears, spread
out my arms, and let them fall in the grass.

I heard someone sob softly from afar. A wind
sprang up and a great mass of leaves, which I
had not seen before, rose rustling into the air.
Unripe fruit thudded senselessly from the trees
onto the ground. Ugly clouds rose from behind
the mountain. The waves on the river creaked
and receded from the wind.

I got up quickly. My heart hurt, for now it
seemed impossible to escape from my suffering.
I was already about to turn and leave this

region and go back to my former way of life when the following idea occurred to me: "How strange it is that even in our time distinguished people are transported across a river in this complicated way. There's no other explanation than that it is an old custom." I shook my head, for I was surprised.

iii *THE FAT MAN*

a An Address to the Landscape

From the thicket on the opposite bank four naked men strode vehemently forth, carrying on their shoulders a wooden litter. On this litter sat, Oriental fashion, a monstrously fat man. Although carried through the thicket on an untrodden path, he did not push the thorny branches apart but simply let his motionless body thrust through them. His folds of fat were so carefully spread out that although they covered the whole litter and even hung down its side like the hem of a yellowish carpet, they did not hamper him. His hairless skull was small and gleamed yellow. His face bore the artless expression of a man who meditates and makes no effort to conceal it. From time to time he closed his eyes: on opening them again his chin became distorted.

"The landscape disturbs my thought," he said in a low voice. "It makes my reflections sway like suspension bridges in a furious current. It is beautiful and for this reason wants to be looked at."

I close my eyes and say: You green mountain by the river, with your rocks rolling against the water, you are beautiful.

But it is not satisfied; it wants me to open my eyes to it.

Then I might say to it with my eyes closed: "Mountain, I do not love you, for you remind me of the clouds, of the sunset, of the rising sky, and these are things that almost make me cry because one can never reach them while being carried on a small litter. But when showing me this, sly mountain, you block the distant view which gladdens me, for it reveals the attainable at a glance. That's why I do not love you, mountain by the water—no, I do not love you."

45

But the mountain would be as indifferent to this speech as to my former one so long as I did not talk with my eyes open. This is the only way to please it.

And must we not keep it well disposed towards us in order to keep it up at all—this mountain which has such a capricious fondness for the pulp of our brains? It might cast on me its jagged shadow, it might silently thrust terrible bare walls in front of me and my bearers would stumble over the little pebbles on the road.

But it is not only the mountain that is so vain, so obtrusive and vindictive—everything else is, too. So I must go on repeating with wide-open eyes—oh, how they hurt!:

"Yes, mountain, you are beautiful and the forests on your western slope delight me.— With you, flower, I am also pleased, and your pink gladdens my soul.—You, grass of the meadows, are already high and strong and refreshing.—And you, exotic bushes, you prick so unexpectedly that our thoughts start leaping.—But with you, river, I am so delighted that I will let myself be carried through your supple water."

After he had shouted this paean of praise ten times, accompanied by some humble shifting of his body, he let his head droop and said with closed eyes:

"But now—I implore you—mountain, flowers, grass, bush, and river, give me some room so that I may breathe."

At that moment the surrounding mountains began to shift in hasty obedience, then withdrew behind a curtain of fog. Although the avenues stood firm for a while and guarded the width of the road, they soon merged into one another. In the sky in front of the sun lay a humid cloud with a delicately transparent edge in whose shade the country sank deeper and deeper while everything else lost its lovely outline.

The sound of the bearers' steps reached my side of the river and yet I could not distinguish any details in the dark square of their faces. I only saw them bending their heads sideways and arching their backs, for their burden was excessive. I was worried about them, for I realized that they were tired. So it was in suspense that I watched them step into the rushes, then walk through the wet sand, their strides still regular, until they finally sank into the muddy swamp where the two rear bearers bent even lower so as to keep the litter in its horizontal position. I pressed my hands together. By now they had to raise their feet high at every step until their bodies glistened with sweat in the cool air of this unsettled afternoon.

The fat man sat quiet, hands on his thighs; the long pointed tips of the reeds grazed him as they flipped up in the wake of the bearers in front.

The bearers' movements grew more irregular the nearer they came to the water. At times the litter swayed as though it were already on the waves. Small puddles in the rushes had to be jumped over or walked around, for they might possibly be deep.

At one moment wild ducks rose shrieking, mounting steeply into the rain cloud. It was then that I caught a glimpse of the fat man's face; it looked alarmed. I got up and in hectic

leaps I zigzagged over the stony slope separating me from the water. I paid no heed to
the danger, was concerned only with helping
the fat man should his servants no longer be
able to carry him. I ran so recklessly that I
couldn't stop, and was forced to dash into the
splashing water, coming to a halt only when
the water reached my knees.

Meanwhile the servants, with considerable
distortions of their bodies, had carried the litter into the river, and holding themselves above
the unruly water with one hand, they propped
up the litter with four hairy arms, their muscles
standing out in relief.

The water lapped against their chins, then
rose to their mouths; the bearers bent their
heads back and the litter-handles fell on their
shoulders. The water was already playing
round the bridges of their noses, and yet they
did not give up, although they had hardly
reached the middle of the river. Then a low
wave swept over the heads of those in front
and the four men drowned in silence, their desperate hands pulling the litter down with them.
Water gushed after them.

And now the evening sun's slanting rays broke forth from behind the rims of the great cloud and illuminated the hills and mountains as far as the eye could see, while the river and the region beneath the cloud lay in an uncertain light.

The fat man turned slowly in the direction of the flowing water and was carried down the river like a yellow wooden idol which had become useless and so had been cast into the river. He sailed along on the reflection of the rain cloud. Elongated clouds pulled and small hunched ones pushed him, creating considerable commotion the effect of which could even be noticed by the lapping of water against my knees and the stones on the shore.

I crept quickly up the slope so as to be able to accompany the fat man on his way, for I truly loved him. And perhaps I could learn something about the dangers of this apparently safe country. So I walked along a strip of sand to the narrowness of which one had to grow accustomed, hands in my pockets and my face turned at right angles to the river so that my chin rested almost on my shoulder.

Swallows sat on the stones by the shore.

The fat man said: "Dear sir on the shore, don't try to rescue me. This is the water's and the wind's revenge; now I am lost. Yes, revenge it is, for how often have we attacked them, I and my friend the supplicant, amidst the singing of our swords, the flash of cymbals, the great splendor of trumpets, and the leaping blaze of drums!"

A tiny mosquito with stretched wings flew straight through his belly without losing its speed.

The fat man continued:

b Beginning of a Conversation with the Supplicant

There was a time when I went to a church day after day, for a girl I was in love with used to kneel there in prayer for half an hour every evening, which enabled me to watch her at my leisure.

Once when the girl failed to appear and in dismay I was watching the other people praying, my eye was caught by a young man who had flung his long emaciated figure on the ground. From time to time he clutched his skull with all his strength and, moaning loudly, beat it in the palms of his hands on the stone floor.

In the church there were only a few old women who kept turning their shawled heads sideways to glance at the praying man. This attention seemed to please him, for before each of his pious outbursts he let his eyes rove about to see how many people were watching him. Finding this unseemly, I decided to accost him on his way out of the church and ask him outright why he prayed in this manner. For since my arrival in this town clarity had become more important to me than anything else, even though at this moment I felt only annoyance at my girl's failure to appear.

Yet an hour passed before he stood up, brushed his trousers for such a long time that I felt like shouting: "Enough, enough! We can all see that you have trousers on," crossed himself carefully, and with the lumbering gait of a sailor walked to the font of holy water.

I placed myself between the font and the

door, determined not to let him pass without an explanation. I screwed up my mouth, this being the best preparation for resolute speech, and supported myself by standing on my right leg while resting the left one on its toes, for this position as I have often experienced gives me a sense of stability.

Now it is possible that this young man had already caught sight of me while sprinkling his face with holy water; perhaps my stare had alarmed him even earlier, for he now quite unexpectedly rushed to the door and out. I involuntarily jumped to stop him. The glass door slammed. And when I passed through it a moment later I could not find him, for the narrow streets were numerous and the traffic considerable.

During the following days he failed to appear, but the girl came and again prayed in a corner of a side chapel. She wore a black dress with a transparent lace yoke—the crescent of her chemise could be seen through it—from the lower edge of which the silk hung down in a finely cut frill. And now that the girl had returned I was glad to forget about the young man, ignoring him even when he continued to appear regularly and to pray in his usual fashion.

Yet he always passed me by in sudden haste, his face averted. While praying, on the other hand, he kept glancing at me. It almost looked as though he were angry with me for not having accosted him earlier and was thinking that by my first attempt to talk to him I had actually taken upon me the duty to do so. One day as I was following the girl out as usual after a service, I ran into him in the semidarkness and thought I saw him smile.

The duty to talk to him, needless to say, did not exist, nor had I much desire to do so any more. And even when I hurried up to the church one evening while the clock was striking seven and found, instead of the girl who of course had left long ago, only the young man exerting himself in front of the altar railings, I still hesitated.

At last I tiptoed to the door, slipped a coin to the blind beggar sitting there, and squeezed in beside him behind the open wing. And there for about half an hour I looked forward to the surprise I was planning to spring upon the supplicant. But this feeling did not last. Before long I was morosely watching spiders creeping over my clothes and finding it tiresome to have to bend forward every time someone came breathing loud out of the darkness of the church.

But finally he came. The ringing of the great bells which had started a little while ago did not agree with him, I realized. Each time before taking a step he had to touch the ground lightly with his foot.

I straightened myself, took a long stride forward, and grabbed him. "Good evening," said I, and with my hand on his coat collar I pushed him down the steps onto the lighted square.

When we had reached ground level he turned towards me while I was still holding on to him from behind, so that we stood breast to breast.

"If only you'd let go of me!" he said. "I don't know what you suspect me of, but I'm innocent." Then he repeated once more: "Of course I don't know what you suspect me of."

55

"There is no question here of suspicion or innocence. I ask you not to mention it again. We are strangers; our acquaintance is no older than the church steps are high. What would happen if we were immediately to start discussing our innocence?"

"Precisely what I think," he said. "As a matter of fact, you said 'our innocence.' Do you mean to suggest that if I had proved my innocence you would have to prove yours, too? Is that what you mean?"

"That or something else," I said. "I accosted you only because I wanted to ask you something, remember that!"

"I'd like to go home," he said, and made an effort to turn.

"I quite believe it. Would I have accosted you otherwise? Don't get the idea that I accosted you on account of your beautiful eyes."

"Aren't you being a little too sincere?"

"Must I repeat that there's no question of such things? What has it to do with sincerity or insincerity? I ask, you answer, and then good-by. So far as I'm concerned you can even go home, and as fast as you like."

"Would it not be better to meet some other time? At a more suitable hour? Say in a coffee-house? Besides, your fiancée left only a few minutes ago, you can easily catch her up, she has waited so long for you."

"No!" I shouted into the noise of the passing tram. "You won't escape me. I like you more and more. You're a lucky catch. I congratulate myself."

To which he said: "Oh God, you have a sound heart, as they say, but a head of wood. You call me a lucky catch, how lucky you must be! For my bad luck is precariously balanced and when touched it falls onto the questioner. And so: Good night."

"Fine," said I, surprised him and seized his right hand. "If you don't answer of your own accord, I'll force you. I'll follow you wherever you go, right or left, even up the stairs to your room, and in your room I'll sit down, wherever there's place. Go on then, keep staring at me, I can stand it. But how"—I stepped up close and because he was a head taller I spoke into his throat—"how are you going to summon up the courage to stop me?"

Whereupon, stepping back, he kissed my hands in turn, and wetted them with his tears. "One cannot deny you anything. Just as you knew I want to go home, I knew even earlier that I cannot deny you anything. All I ask is that we go over there into the side street." I nodded and we went over. When a carriage separated us and I was left behind, he beckoned to me with both hands, to make me hurry.

But once there, not satisfied with the darkness of the street where the lamps were widely separated from one another and almost as high as the first floor, he led me into the low hallway of an old house and under a small lamp which hung dripping in front of the wooden stairs.

Spreading his handkerchief over the hollow in a worn step, he invited me to be seated: "It's easier for you to ask questions sitting down. I'll remain standing, it's easier for me to answer. But don't torment me!"

I sat down because he took it all so seriously, but nevertheless felt I had to say: "You've led me to this hole as though we are conspirators, whereas I am bound to you simply by curiosity, you to me by fear. Actually, all I want to ask is why you pray like that in church. The way you carry on there! Like an utter fool! How ridiculous it all is, how unpleasant for the onlookers, how intolerable for the devout!"

He had pressed his body against the wall, only his head moved slowly in space. "You're wrong! The devout consider my behavior natural, the others consider it devout."

"My annoyance proves you're mistaken."

"Your annoyance—assuming it's real—only proves that you belong neither to the devout nor to the others."

"You're right. I was exaggerating when I said your behavior annoyed me; no, it aroused my curiosity as I stated correctly at first. But you, to which group do you belong?"

"Oh, I just get fun out of people watching me, out of occasionally casting a shadow on the altar, so to speak."

"Fun?" I asked, making a face.

"No, if you want to know. Don't be angry with me for expressing it wrongly. It's not fun, for me it's a need; a need to let myself be nailed down for a brief hour by those eyes, while the whole town around me——''

"The things you say!" I cried far too loud for the insignificant remark and the low hallway, but I was afraid of falling silent or of lowering my voice. "Really, the things you say! Now I realize, by God, that I guessed from the very beginning the state you are in. Isn't it something like a fever, a seasickness on land, a kind of leprosy? Don't you feel it's this very feverishness which is preventing you from being properly satisfied with the real names of things, and that now, in your frantic haste, you're just pelting them with any old names? You can't do it fast enough. But hardly have you run away from them when you've forgotten the names you gave them. The poplar in the fields, which you've called the 'Tower of Babel' because you didn't want to know it was a poplar, sways again without a name, so you have to call it 'Noah in his cups.' ''

He interrupted me: "I'm glad I haven't understood a word you've been saying."

Irritated, I said quickly: "Your being glad

about it proves that you have understood it."

"Didn't I say so before? One cannot deny you anything."

I put my hands on a step above me, leaned back, and in this all but unassailable position, the wrestler's last resort, I asked: "Excuse me, but to throw back at me an explanation which I gave you is insincere."

At this he grew daring. To give his body unity he clasped his hands together and said with some reluctance: "You ruled out quarrels about insincerity from the very beginning. And truly, I'm no longer concerned with anything but to give you a proper explanation for my way of praying. Do you know why I pray like that?"

He was putting me to the test. No, I didn't know, nor did I want to know. I hadn't even wanted to come here, I said to myself, but this creature had practically forced me to listen to him. So all I had to do was to shake my head and everything would be all right, but at the moment this was just what I couldn't do. The creature opposite me smiled. Then he crouched down on his knees and said with a sleepy expression: "Now I can also tell you at last why I let you accost me. Out of curiosity, from hope. Your stare has been comforting me for a long time. And I hope to learn from you how things really are, why it is that around me things sink away like fallen snow, whereas for other people even a little liqueur glass stands on the table steady as a statue."

As I remained silent and only an involuntary twitching passed over my face, he asked: "So you don't believe this happens to other people? You really don't? Just listen, then. When as a child I opened my eyes after a brief afternoon nap, still not quite sure I was alive, I heard my mother up on the balcony asking in a natural tone of voice: 'What are you doing, my dear? Goodness, isn't it hot?' From the garden a woman answered: 'Me, I'm having my tea on the lawn.' They spoke casually and not very distinctly, as though this woman had expected the question, my mother the answer."

Feeling that this required an answer, I put my hand in the hip pocket of my trousers as though I were looking for something. Actually, I wasn't looking for anything, I just wished to

change my appearance in order to show interest in the conversation. Finally I said I
thought this a most remarkable incident and
that I couldn't make head or tail of it. I also
added that I didn't believe it was true and
that it must have been invented for a special
reason whose purpose wasn't clear to me just
now. Then I closed my eyes so as to shut out
the bad light.

"Well, isn't that encouraging! For once you
agree with me, and you accosted me to tell me
that out of sheer unselfishness. I lose one hope
and acquire another.

"Why, after all, should I feel ashamed of
not walking upright and taking normal steps,
of not tapping the pavement with my stick, and
not touching the clothes of the people who
pass noisily by? Am I not rather entitled to
complain bitterly at having to skip along the
houses like a shadow without a clear outline,
sometimes disappearing in the panes of the
shop windows?

"Oh, what dreadful days I have to live
through! Why is everything so badly built that
high houses collapse every now and again

for no apparent reason? On these occasions I clamber over the rubble, asking everyone I meet: 'How could this have happened? In our town—a new house—how many does that make today?——Just think of it!' And no one can give me an answer.

"Frequently people fall in the street and lie there dead. Whereupon all the shop people open their doors laden with wares, hurry busily out, cart the dead into a house, come out again all smiles, then the chatter begins: 'Good morning—it's a dull day—I'm selling any amount of kerchiefs—ah yes, the war.' I rush into the house, and after raising my hand several times timidly with my finger crooked, I finally knock on the janitor's little window: 'Good morning,' I say, 'I understand a dead man was carried in here just now. Would you be kind enough to let me see him?' And when he shakes his head as though unable to make up his mind, I add: 'Take care, I'm a member of the secret police and insist on seeing the dead man at once!' Now he is no longer undecided. 'Out with you!' he shouts. 'This riffraff is getting in the habit of snooping about here every day. There's no dead man here. Maybe next door.' I raise my hat and go.

"But then, on having to cross a large square, I forget everything. If people must build such huge squares from sheer wantonness, why don't they build a balustrade across them as well? Today there's a southwest wind blowing. The spire of the Town Hall is moving in little circles. All the windowpanes are rattling, and the lampposts are bending like bamboos. The Virgin Mary's cloak is coiling round her pillar and the wind is tugging at it. Does no one notice this? The ladies and gentlemen who should be walking on the pavement are floating. When the wind falls they stand still, say a few words, and bow to one another, but when the wind rises again they are helpless, and all their feet leave the ground at the same time. Although obliged to hold on to their hats, their eyes twinkle gaily enough and no one has the slightest fault to find with the weather. I'm the only one who's afraid."

To which I was able to say: "That story you told me earlier about your mother and the woman in the garden I really don't find so remarkable. Not only have I heard and experienced many stories of this kind, I have even taken part in some. The whole thing is perfectly natural. Do you really mean to suggest that had I been on that balcony in the summer, I could not have asked the same question and given the same answer from the garden? Quite an ordinary occurrence!"

After I had said this, he seemed relieved at last. He told me I was well dressed and that he very much liked my tie. And what a fine complexion I had. And that confessions became most comprehensible when they were retracted.

c The Supplicant's Story

Then he sat down beside me, for I had grown timid and, bending my head to one side, had made room for him. Nevertheless, it didn't escape my notice that he too was sitting there rather embarrassed, trying to keep some distance from me and speaking with difficulty:

"Oh, what dreadful days I have to live through! Last night I was at a party. I was just bowing to a young lady in the gaslight and saying: 'I'm so glad winter's approaching'—I was just bowing with these words when to my annoyance I noticed that my right thigh had slipped out of joint. The kneecap had also become a little loose.

"So I sat down, and as I always try to keep control over my sentences, I said: 'for winter's much less of an effort; it's easier to comport oneself, one doesn't have to take so much trouble with one's words. Don't you agree, Fräulein? I do hope I'm right about this.' My right leg was now giving me a lot of trouble. At first it seemed to have fallen apart completely, and only gradually did I manage to get it more or less back into shape by manipulation and careful rearrangement.

"Then I heard the girl, who, out of sympathy, had also sat down, say in a low voice: 'No, you don't impress me at all because——'

" 'Just a moment,' I said, pleased and full of expectation, 'you mustn't waste so much as five minutes talking to me, dear Fräulein. Please eat something while you're talking, I implore you.'

"And stretching out my arm I took a large

bunch of grapes hanging heavily from a bowl held up by a bronze winged cupid, dangled it for a moment in the air, and then laid it on a small blue plate which I handed to the girl, not without a certain elegance, I trust.

" 'You don't impress me at all,' she said, 'everything you say is boring and incomprehensible, but that alone doesn't make it true. What I really think, sir—why do you always call me dear Fräulein?—is that you can't be bothered with the truth simply because it's too tiring.'

"God, how good that made me feel! 'Yes, Fräulein, Fräulein!' I almost shouted, 'how right you are! Dear Fräulein, if you only knew what a wild joy it is to find oneself so well understood—and without having made any effort!'

" 'There's no doubt, sir, that for you the truth is too tiring. Just look at yourself! The entire length of you is cut out of tissue paper, yellow tissue paper, like a silhouette, and when you walk one ought to hear you rustle. So one shouldn't get annoyed at your attitude

68

or opinion, for you can't help bending to whatever draft happens to be in the room.'

" 'I don't understand that. True, several people are standing about here in this room. They lay their arms on the backs of chairs or they lean against the piano or they raise a glass tentatively to their mouths or they walk timidly into the next room, and having knocked their right shoulders against a cupboard in the dark, they stand breathing by the open window and think: There's Venus, the evening star. Yet here I am, among them. If there is a connection, I don't understand it. But I don't even know if there is a connection. —And you see, dear Fräulein, of all these people who behave so irresolutely, so absurdly as a result of their confusion, I alone seem worthy of hearing the truth about myself. And to make this truth more palatable you put it in a mocking way so that something concrete remains, like the outer walls of a house whose interior has been gutted. The eye is hardly obstructed; by day the clouds and sky can be seen through the great window holes, and by night the stars. But the clouds are often hewn out of gray stones, and the stars form unnatural constellations.—How would it be if in return I were to tell you that one day everyone wanting to live will look like me—cut out of tissue paper, like silhouettes, as you pointed out —and when they walk they will be heard to rustle? Not that they will be any different from what they are now, but that is what they will look like. Even you, dear Fräulein——'

"Then I noticed that the girl was no longer sitting beside me. She must have left soon after her last words, for now she was standing far away from me by a window, surrounded by three young men who were talking and laughing out of high white collars.

"So I happily drank a glass of wine and walked over to the pianist who, all alone and nodding to himself, happened to be playing something sad. I bent carefully down to his ear so as not to frighten him and whispered into the melody: 'Be so kind, sir, as to let me play now, for I'm just beginning to feel happy.'

"Since he paid no attention to me, I stood

there for a while embarrassed, but then, over-
coming my timidity, I went from one guest to
another, saying casually: 'Today I'm going to
play the piano. Yes.'

"Everyone seemed to know I couldn't play,
but they smiled in a friendly way, pleased by
the welcome interruption of their conversation.
They paid proper attention to me only when I
said to the pianist in a very loud voice: 'Do
me the favor, sir, of letting me play now. After
all, I'm just beginning to feel happy. A tri-
umph is at stake.'

"Although the pianist stopped, he neither
left his brown bench nor appeared to understand me. He sighed and covered his face with
his long fingers.

"I felt a trifle sorry for him and was about to
encourage him to continue playing when the
hostess approached with a group of people.

" 'That's a funny coincidence,' they said and
laughed aloud as though I were about to do
something unnatural.

"The girl also joined them, looked at me
contemptuously, and said: 'Please, madame,

71

do let him play. Perhaps he wants to make some contribution to the entertainment. He ought to be encouraged. Please let him.'

"Everyone laughed, obviously thinking, as I did, that it was meant ironically. Only the pianist was silent. Holding his head low, he stroked the wood of the bench with the forefinger of his left hand, as though he were making designs in sand. I began to tremble, and to hide it thrust my hands into my trouser pockets. Nor could I speak clearly any longer, for my whole face wanted to cry. Thus I had to choose the words in such a way that the thought of my wanting to cry would appear ludicrous to the listeners.

" 'Madame,' I said, 'I must play now because——' As I had forgotten the reason I abruptly sat down at the piano. And then I remembered again. The pianist stood up and stepped tactfully over the bench, for I was blocking his way. 'Please turn out the light, I can only play in the dark.' I straightened myself.

"At that moment two gentlemen seized the

72

bench and, whistling a song and rocking me to and fro, carried me far away from the piano to the dining table.

"Everyone watched with approval and the girl said: 'You see, madame, he played quite well. I knew he would. And you were so worried.'

"I understood and thanked her with a bow, which I carried out well.

"They poured me some lemonade and a girl with red lips held my glass while I drank. The hostess offered me a meringue on a silver salver and a girl in a pure white dress put the meringue in my mouth. Another girl, voluptuous and with a mass of fair hair, held a bunch of grapes over me, and all I had to do was pluck them off with my lips while she gazed into my receding eyes.

"Since everyone was treating me so well I was a little surprised that they were so unanimous in holding me back when I tried to return to the piano.

" 'That's enough now,' said the host, whom I had not noticed before. He went out and promptly returned with an enormous top hat and a copper-brown overcoat with a flowery design. 'Here are your things.'

"They weren't my things, of course, but I didn't want to put him to the trouble of looking again. The host helped me into the overcoat which fitted beautifully, clinging tightly to my thin body. Bending over slowly, a lady with a kind face buttoned the coat all the way down.

" 'Good-by,' said the hostess, 'and come back soon. You know you're always welcome.' Whereupon everyone bowed as though they thought it necessary. I tried to do likewise, but my coat was too tight. So I took my hat and, no doubt awkwardly, walked out of the room.

"But as I passed through the front door with short steps I was assaulted from the sky by moon and stars and a great vaulted expanse, and from the Ringplatz by the Town Hall, the Virgin's pillar, the church.

"I walked calmly from the shadow into the moonlight, unbuttoned my overcoat, and warmed myself; then I put a stop to the humming of the night by raising my hands, and began to reflect as follows:

" 'What is it that makes you all behave as though you were real? Are you trying to make me believe I'm unreal, standing here absurdly on the green pavement? You, sky, surely it's a long time since you've been real, and as for you, Ringplatz, you never have been real.

" 'It's true, you're all still superior to me, but only when I leave you alone.

" 'Thank God, moon, you are no longer moon, but perhaps it's negligent of me to go on calling you so-called moon, moon. Why do your spirits fall when I call you "forgotten paper lantern of a strange color"? And why do you almost withdraw when I call you "the Virgin's pillar"? As for you, pillar of the Virgin Mary, I hardly recognize your threatening attitude when I call you "moon shedding yellow light."

" 'It really seems to me that thinking about you doesn't do you any good; you lose in courage and health.

" 'God, how much more profitable it would

be if the Thinker could learn from the Drunk!

" 'Why has everything become so quiet? I think the wind has dropped. And the small houses which often used to roll across the square as though on little wheels are rooted to the spot—calm—calm—one can't even see the thin black line that used to separate them from the ground.'

"And I started to run. I ran unimpeded three times round the great square, and as I didn't meet a drunk I ran on towards the Karlsgasse without slowing down and without any effort. My shadow, often smaller than myself, ran beside me along the wall as though in a gorge between the wall and the street level.

"As I passed the fire station I heard a noise coming from the Kleiner Ring, and as I turned into it I saw a drunk standing by the iron railing of the fountain, his arms held out sideways and his feet in wooden shoes stamping the ground.

"Stopping to get my breath, I went up to him, raised my top hat, and introduced myself:

" 'Good evening, gentle nobleman, I am twenty-three years of age, but as yet I have no name. But you, no doubt, hail from the great city of Paris—bearing extraordinary, well-nigh singable names. You are surrounded by the quite unnatural odor of the dissolute Court of France. No doubt your tinted eyes have beheld those great ladies standing on the high shining terrace ironically twisting their narrow waists while the ends of their decorated trains, spread over the steps, are still lying on the sand in the garden.—And surely, menservants in daringly cut gray tailcoats and white knee breeches climb tall poles, their legs hugging them but their torsos frequently bent back and to the side, for they have to raise enormous gray linen sheets off the ground with thick ropes and spread them in the air, because the great lady has expressed the wish for a misty morning.'

"When he belched I felt almost frightened. 'Is it really true, sir,' I said, 'that you hail from our Paris, from that tempestuous Paris—ah, from that luxuriant hailstorm?'

77

"When he belched again, I said with em-
barrassment: 'I know, a great honor is being
bestowed upon me.'

"And with nimble fingers I buttoned up my
overcoat; then with ardor and yet timidly I
said: 'I know you do not consider me worthy
of an answer, but if I did not ask you today
my life would be spent in weeping. I ask you,
much-bespangled sir, is it true what I have
been told? Are there people in Paris who con-
sist only of sumptuous dresses, and are there
houses that are only portals, and is it true that
on summer days the sky over the city is a
fleeting blue embellished only by little white
clouds glued onto it, all in the shape of hearts?
And have they a highly popular panopticon
there containing nothing but trees to which
small plaques are fastened bearing the names
of the most famous heroes, criminals, and lovers?

" 'And then this other piece of news! This
clearly fabricated news! These Paris streets,
for instance, they suddenly branch off, don't
they? They're turbulent, aren't they? Things
are not always as they should be, how could

78

they be, after all? Sometimes there's an accident, people gather together from the side streets with that urban stride that hardly touches the pavement; they are all filled with curiosity, but also with fear of disappointment; they breathe fast and stretch out their little heads. But when they touch one another they bow low and apologize: "I'm awfully sorry—I didn't mean it—there's such a crowd; forgive me, I beg you—it was most clumsy of me, I admit. My name is—my name's Jerome Faroche, I'm a grocer in the rue de Cabotin—allow me to invite you to lunch tomorrow—my wife would also be delighted."

" 'So they go on talking while the street lies numb and the smoke from the chimneys falls between the houses. That's how it is. But it might happen that two carriages stop on a crowded boulevard of a distinguished neighborhood. Serious-looking menservants open the doors. Eight elegant Siberian wolfhounds come prancing out and jump barking across the boulevard. And it's said that they are young Parisian dandies in disguise.'

"His eyes were almost shut. When I fell si-

lent, he stuck both hands in his mouth and tore
at his lower jaw. His clothes were covered with
dirt. Perhaps he had been thrown out of some
tavern and hadn't yet realized it.

"Perhaps it was that short quiet lull between
night and day when our heads loll back unexpectedly, when everything stands still without
our knowing it, since we are not looking at it,
and then disappears; we remain alone, our
bodies bent, then look round but no longer see
anything, nor even feel any resistance in the
air yet inwardly we cling to the memory that
at a certain distance from us stand houses
with roofs and with fortunately angular chimneys down which the darkness flows through
garrets into various rooms. And it is fortunate
that tomorrow will be a day on which, unlikely
as it may seem, one will be able to see everything.

"Now the drunk jerked up his eyebrows so
that a brightness appeared between them and
his eyes, and he explained in fits and starts:
'It's like this, you see—I'm sleepy, you see, so
that's why I'm going to sleep.—You see, I've a
brother-in-law on the Wenzelsplatz—that's

where I'm going, for I live there, for that's where I have my bed—so I'll be off—. But I don't know his name, you see, or where he lives —seems I've forgotten—but never mind, for I don't even know if I have a brother-in-law at all.—But I'll be off now, you see—. Do you think I'll find him?'

"To which, without thinking, I said: 'That's certain. But you're coming from abroad and your servants don't happen to be with you. Allow me to show you the way.'

"He didn't answer. So I offered him my arm, to give him some support."

d Continued Conversation Between the Fat Man and the Supplicant

For some time already I had been trying to cheer myself up. I rubbed my body and said to myself: "It's time you spoke. You're becoming embarrassed. Do you feel oppressed? Just wait! You know these situations. Think it over at your leisure. Even the landscape will wait.

"It's the same as it was at the party last week. Someone is reading aloud from a manu-

81

script. At his request I myself have copied one page. When I see my handwriting among the pages written by him, I take fright. It's without any stability. People are bending over it from three sides of the table. In tears, I swear it's not my handwriting."

"But what is the connection with today? It's entirely up to you to start a sensible conversation. Everything's peaceful. Just make an effort, my friend! —You surely can find an objection. —You can say: 'I'm sleepy. I've a headache. Good-by.' Quick then, quick! Make yourself conspicuous!—What's that? Again obstacles and more obstacles? What does it remind you of?—I remember a high plateau which rose against the wide sky as a shield to the earth. I saw it from a mountain and prepared myself to wander through it. I began to sing."

My lips were dry and disobedient as I said: "Ought it not to be possible to live differently?"

"No," he said, questioning, smiling.

"But why do you pray in church every evening?" I asked then, while everything between

him and me, which until then I had been holding together as though in my sleep, collapsed.

"Oh, why should we talk about it? People
who live alone have no responsibility in the
evenings. One fears a number of things—that
one's body could vanish, that human beings
may really be what they appear to be at twi-
light, that one might not be allowed to walk
without a stick, that it might be a good idea to
go to church and pray at the top of one's voice
in order to be looked at and acquire a body."

Because he talked like that and then fell silent, I pulled my red handkerchief out of my
pocket, bent my head, and wept.

He stood up, kissed me, and said: "What
are you crying for? You're tall, I like that; you
have long hands which all but obey your will;
why aren't you happy about it? Always wear
dark cuffs, that's my advice. —No—I flatter
you and yet you cry? I think you cope quite
sensibly with the difficulty of living."

"We build useless war machines, towers,
walls, curtains of silk, and we could marvel at
all this a great deal if we had the time. We
tremble in the balance, we don't fall, we flutter,

even though we may be uglier than bats. And on a beautiful day hardly anyone can prevent us from saying: 'Oh God, today is a beautiful day,' for we are already established on this Earth and live by virtue of an agreement.

"For we are like tree trunks in the snow. They lie there apparently flat on the ground and it looks as though one could push them away with a slight kick. But no, one can't, for they are firmly stuck to the ground. So you see even this is only apparent."

The following thought prevented me from sobbing: "It is night and no one will reproach me tomorrow for what I might say now, for it could have been said in my sleep."

Then I said: "Yes, that's it, but what were we talking about? We can't have been talking about the light in the sky because we are standing in the darkness of a hallway. No—we could have talked about it, nevertheless, for are we not free to say what we like in conversation? After all, we're not aiming at any definite purpose or at the truth, but simply at making jokes and having a good time. Even so, couldn't you tell me the story of the woman in the garden once more? How admirable, how clever this woman is! We must follow her example. How fond I am of her! So it's a good thing I met you and waylaid you as I did. It has given me great pleasure to talk to you. I've learned several things that, perhaps intentionally, were hitherto unknown to me.—I'm grateful."

He looked pleased. And although contact with a human body is always repugnant to me, I couldn't help embracing him.

Then we stepped out of the hallway under the sky. My friend blew away a few bruised little clouds, allowing the uninterrupted surface of the stars to emerge. He walked with difficulty.

iv *DROWNING OF THE FAT MAN*

And now everything was seized by speed and fell into the distance. The water of the river was dragged towards a precipice, tried to resist, whirled about a little at the crumbling edge, but then crashed in foaming smoke.

The fat man could not go on talking, he was

forced to turn and disappear in the loud roar of the waterfall.

I, who had experienced so many pleasant diversions, stood on the bank and watched. "What are our lungs supposed to do?" I shouted. Shouted: "If they breathe fast they suffocate themselves from inner poisons; if they breathe slowly they suffocate from unbreathable air, from outraged things. But if they try to search for their own rhythm they perish from the mere search."

Meanwhile the banks of the river stretched beyond all bounds, and yet with the palm of my hand I touched the metal of a signpost which gleamed minutely in the far distance. This I really couldn't quite understand. After all I was small, almost smaller than usual, and a bush of white heps shaking itself very fast towered over me. This I saw, for a moment ago it had been close to me.

Nevertheless I was mistaken, for my arms were as huge as the clouds of a steady country rain, save that they were more hasty. I don't know why they were trying to crush my poor head. It was no larger than an ant's egg, but slightly damaged, and as a result no longer quite round. I made some beseeching, twisting movements with it, for the expression of my eyes could not have been noticed, they were so small.

But my legs, my impossible legs lay over the wooded mountains and gave shade to the village-studded valleys. They grew and grew! They already reached into the space that no longer owned any landscape, for some time their length had gone beyond my field of vision.

But no, it isn't like that—after all, I'm small, small for the time being—I'm rolling—I'm rolling—I'm an avalanche in the mountains! Please, passers-by, be so kind as to tell me how tall I am—just measure these arms, these legs.

III

"Let me think," said my acquaintance, who had accompanied me from the party and was walking quietly beside me on a path up the Laurenziberg. "Just stand still a moment so that I can get it clear.—I have something to settle, you know. It's all such a strain—the night is radiant, though rather cold, but this discontented wind, it sometimes even seems to change the position of those acacias."

The moon made the gardener's house cast a shadow over the slightly humped path on which lay scanty patches of snow. When I saw the bench that stood beside the door, I pointed at it with a raised finger, and as I was not brave and expected reproaches I laid my left hand on my chest.

He sat down wearily, disregarding his beautiful clothes, and astonished me by pressing his elbows against his hips and laying his forehead on the tips of his overstretched fingers.

"Yes, now I want to say this. You know, I live a regular life. No fault can be found with it, everything I do is considered correct and generally approved. Misfortune, as it is known in the society I frequent, has not spared me, as my surroundings and I have realized with satisfaction, and even the general good fortune has not failed me and I myself have been able to talk about it in a small circle of friends. True, until now I had never been really in love.

I regretted it occasionally, but used the phrase when I needed it. And now I must confess: Yes, I am in love and quite beside myself with excitement. I am an ardent lover, just what the girls dream of. But ought I not to have considered that just this former lack of mine gave an exceptional and gay, an especially gay, twist to my circumstances?"

"Calm yourself," I said without interest, thinking only of myself. "Your loved one is beautiful, as I couldn't help hearing."

"Yes, she is beautiful. While sitting next to her, all I could think was: What an adventure —am I not daring!—there I go embarking on a sea voyage—drinking wine by the gallon. But when she laughs she doesn't show her teeth as one would expect; instead, all one sees is the dark, narrow, curved opening of the mouth. Now this looks sly and senile, even though she throws back her head while laughing."

"I can't deny that," I said, sighing. "I've probably seen it, too, for it must be conspicuous. But it's not only that. It's the beauty of girls altogether. Often when I see dresses with manifold pleats, frills and flounces smoothly

89

clinging to beautiful bodies, it occurs to me that they will not remain like this for long, that they will get creases that cannot be ironed out, dust will gather in the trimmings too thick to be removed, and that no one will make herself so miserable and ridiculous as every day to put on the same precious dress in the morning and take it off at night. And yet I see girls who are beautiful enough, displaying all kinds of attractive muscles and little bones and smooth skin and masses of fine hair, and who appear every day in the same natural fancy dress, always laying the same face in the same palm and letting it be reflected in the mirror. Only sometimes at night, on returning late from a party, this face stares out at them from the mirror worn out, swollen, already seen by too many people, hardly worth wearing any more."

"I've asked you several times on our walk whether you found my girl beautiful, but you always turned away without answering. Tell me, are you up to some mischief? Why don't you comfort me?"

I dug my feet into the shadow and said

kindly: "You don't need to be comforted. After all, you're being loved." To avoid catching cold I held over my mouth a handkerchief with a design of blue grapes.

Now he turned towards me and leaned his fat face against the low back of the bench: "Actually I've still time, you know. I can still end this budding love affair at once, either by committing some misdeed, by unfaithfulness, or by going off to some distant land. For I've grave doubts about whether I should let myself in for all this excitement. Nothing is certain, no one can tell the direction or the duration for sure. If I go into a tavern with the intention of getting drunk, I know I'll be drunk that evening. But in this case! In a week's time we're planning to go on an excursion with some friends. Imagine the storm this will create in the heart for the next fortnight! Last night's kisses make me sleepy and prepare the way for savage dreams. I fight this by going for a walk at night, with the result that I'm in a permanent state of turmoil, my face goes hot and cold as though blown about by the wind, I have to keep fingering a pink ribbon in my pocket all the time, I'm filled with the gravest apprehensions about myself which I cannot follow up, and I can even stand your company, sir, whereas normally I would never spend so much time talking to you."

I was feeling very cold and the sky was already turning a whitish color. "I'm afraid no misdeed, no unfaithfulness or departure to some distant land will be of any avail. You'll have to kill yourself," I said, adding a smile.

Opposite us on the other side of the avenue stood two bushes and down below these bushes was the town. There were still a few lights on.

"All right," he cried, and hit the bench with his little tight fist which, however, he left lying there. "But you go on living. You don't kill yourself. No one loves you. You don't achieve anything. You can't cope with the next moment. Yet you dare to talk to me like that, you brute. You're incapable of loving, only fear excites you. Just take a look at my chest."

Whereupon he quickly opened his overcoat and waistcoat and his shirt. His chest was indeed broad and beautiful.

"Yes, such obstinate moods come over one sometimes," I began to say. "This summer I was in a village which lay by a river. I remember it well. I frequently sat on a bench by the shore in a twisted position. There was a hotel, and one often heard the sound of violins. Young healthy people sat in the garden at tables with beer and talked of hunting and adventures. And on the other shore were cloudlike mountains."

Then, with a limp, distorted mouth, I got up, stepped onto the lawn behind the bench, broke a few snow-covered twigs, and whispered into my acquaintance's ear: "I'm engaged, I confess it."

My acquaintance wasn't surprised that I had got up. "You're engaged?" He sat there really quite exhausted, supported only by the back of the bench. Then he took off his hat and I saw his hair which, scented and beautifully combed, set off the round head on a fleshy neck in a sharp curving line, as was the fashion that winter.

I was pleased to have answered him so cleverly. "Just think," I said to myself, "how he moves in society with flexible neck and free-swinging arms. Keeping up an intelligent conversation, he can steer a lady right through a drawing room, and the fact that it's raining outside, that some timid man is standing about or some other wretched thing is happening, does not make him nervous. No, he goes on bowing with the same courtesy to the ladies. And there he sits now."

My acquaintance mopped his brow with a batiste handkerchief. "Please put your hand on my forehead," he said. "I beg you." When I didn't do so at once, he folded his hands.

As though our sorrow had darkened everything, we sat high up on the mountain as in a small room, although a little earlier we had already noticed the light and wind of the morning. We sat close together in spite of not liking one another at all, but we couldn't move far apart because the walls were firmly and definitely drawn. We could, however, behave absurdly and without human dignity, for we didn't have to be ashamed in the presence of the branches above us and the trees standing opposite us.

Then, without further ado, my acquaintance pulled a knife out of his pocket, opened it thoughtfully, and then, as though he were playing, he plunged it into his left upper arm, and didn't withdraw it. Blood promptly began to flow. His round cheeks grew pale. I pulled out the knife, cut up the sleeve of his overcoat and jacket, tore his shirt sleeve open. Then I ran a little way up and down the road to see if there was anyone who could help. All the branches were almost exaggeratedly visible and motionless. I sucked a little at the deep wound. Then I remembered the gardener's cottage. I ran up the steps leading to the upper lawn on the left side of the house, quickly examined the windows and doors, rang the bell furiously and stamped my feet, although I knew all the time that the house was uninhabited. Then I looked at the wound which was bleeding in a thin trickle. Having wetted his handkerchief in snow, I tied it clumsily round his arm.

"My dear, dear friend," said I, "you've wounded yourself for my sake. You're in such a good position, you're surrounded by well-meaning friends, you can go for a walk in broad daylight when any number of carefully dressed people can be seen far and near among tables or on mountain paths. Just think, in the spring we'll drive into the orchard—no, not we, that's unfortunately true—but you with your Annie will drive out at a happy trot. Oh yes, believe me, I beg you, and the sun will show you off to everyone at your best. Oh, there'll be music, the sound of horses from afar, no need to worry, there'll be shouting and barrel organs will be playing in the avenues."

"Oh God," he said, stood up, leaned on me and we went on, "oh God, that won't help. That won't make me happy. Excuse me. Is it late? Perhaps I ought to do something in the morning. Oh God."

A lantern was burning close to the wall above; it threw the shadows of the tree trunks across the road and the white snow, while on the slope the shadows of all the branches lay bent, as though broken.

BLUMFELD,
AN ELDERLY
BACHELOR

One evening Blumfeld, an elderly bachelor, was climbing up to his apartment—a laborious undertaking, for he lived on the sixth floor. While climbing up he thought, as he had so often recently, how unpleasant this utterly lonely life was: to reach his empty rooms he had to climb these six floors almost in secret, there put on his dressing gown, again almost in secret, light his pipe, read a little of the French magazine to which he had been subscribing for years, at the same time sip at a homemade kirsch, and finally, after half an hour, go to bed, but not before having completely rearranged his bedclothes which the unteachable charwoman would insist on arranging in her own way. Some companion, someone to witness these activities, would have been very welcome to Blumfeld. He had already been wondering whether he shouldn't acquire a little dog. These animals are gay and above all grateful and loyal;

one of Blumfeld's colleagues has a dog of this kind; it follows no one but its master and when it hasn't seen him for a few moments it greets him at once with loud barkings, by which it is evidently trying to express its joy at once more finding that extraordinary bene-factor, its master. True, a dog also has its drawbacks. However well kept it may be, it is bound to dirty the room. This just cannot be avoided; one cannot give it a hot bath each time before letting it into the room; be-sides, its health couldn't stand that. Blumfeld, on the other hand, can't stand dirt in his room. To him cleanliness is essential, and sev-eral times a week he is obliged to have words with his charwoman, who is unfortunately not very painstaking in this respect. Since she is hard of hearing he usually drags her by the arm to those spots in the room which he finds lacking in cleanliness. By this strict discipline he has achieved in his room a neatness more or less commensurate with his wishes. By ac-quiring a dog, however, he would be almost deliberately introducing into his room the dirt which hitherto he had been so careful to avoid. Fleas, the dog's constant companions, would appear. And once fleas were there, it would not be long before Blumfeld would be abandoning his comfortable room to the dog and looking for another one. Uncleanliness, however, is but one of the drawbacks of dogs. Dogs also fall ill and no one really understands dogs' diseases. Then the animal sits in a corner or limps about, whimpers, coughs, chokes from some pain; one wraps it in a rug, whistles a little melody, offers it milk—in short, one nurses it in the hope that this, as indeed is possible, is a passing sickness while it may be a serious, disgusting, and contagious disease. And even if the dog remains healthy, one day it will grow old, one won't have the heart to get rid of the faithful animal in time, and then comes the moment when one's own age peers out at one from the dog's oozing eyes. Then one has to cope with the half-blind, weak-lunged animal all but immobile with fat, and in this way pay dearly for the pleasures the dog once had given. Much as Blumfeld would like to have a dog at this moment, he would rather go on climbing the stairs alone for another thirty years than be burdened later on by such an old dog which, sighing louder than he, would drag itself up, step by step.

So Blumfeld will remain alone, after all; he really feels none of the old maid's longing to have around her some submissive living creature that she can protect, lavish her affection upon, and continue to serve—for which purpose a cat, a canary, even a goldfish would suffice—or, if this cannot be, rest content with flowers on the windowsill. Blumfeld only wants a companion, an animal to which he doesn't have to pay much attention, which doesn't mind an occasional kick, which even, in an emergency, can spend the night in the street, but which nevertheless, when Blumfeld feels like it, is promptly at his disposal with its barking, jumping, and licking of hands. This is what Blumfeld wants, but since, as he realizes, it cannot be had without serious drawbacks, he renounces it, and yet—in accordance with his thoroughgoing disposition —the idea from time to time, this evening, for instance, occurs to him again.

While taking the key from his pocket outside his room, he is startled by a sound coming from within. A peculiar rattling sound,
very lively but very regular. Since Blumfeld
has just been thinking of dogs, it reminds him
of the sounds produced by paws pattering
one after the other over a floor. But paws don't
rattle, so it can't be paws. He quickly unlocks
the door and switches on the light. He is not
prepared for what he sees. For this is magic—
two small white celluloid balls with blue
stripes jumping up and down side by side on
the parquet; when one of them touches the
floor the other is in the air, a game they continue ceaselessly to play. At school one day
Blumfeld had seen some little pellets jumping
about like this during a well-known electrical
experiment, but these are comparatively large
balls jumping freely about in the room and no
electrical experiment is being made. Blumfeld
bends down to get a good look at them. They
are undoubtedly ordinary balls, they probably
contain several smaller balls, and it is these
which produce the rattling sound. Blumfeld
gropes in the air to find out whether they are

hanging from some threads—no, they are moving entirely on their own. A pity Blumfeld isn't a small child, two balls like these would have been a happy surprise for him, whereas now the whole thing gives him rather an unpleasant feeling. It's not quite pointless after all to live in secret as an unnoticed bachelor, now someone, no matter who, has penetrated this secret and sent him these two strange balls.

He tries to catch one but they retreat before him, thus luring him on to follow them through the room. It's really too silly, he thinks, running after balls like this; he stands still and realizes that the moment he abandons the pursuit, they too remain on the same spot. I will try to catch them all the same, he thinks again, and hurries towards them. They immediately run away, but Blumfeld, his legs apart, forces them into a corner of the room, and there, in front of a trunk, he manages to catch one ball. It's a small cool ball, and it turns in his hand, clearly anxious to slip away. And the other ball, too, as though aware of its comrade's distress, jumps higher than before, extending the leaps until it touches

Blumfeld's hand. It beats against his hand, beats in ever faster leaps, alters its angle of attack, then, powerless against the hand which encloses the ball so completely, springs even higher and is probably trying to reach Blumfeld's face. Blumfeld could catch this ball too, and lock them both up somewhere, but at the moment it strikes him as too humiliating to take such measures against two little balls. Besides, it's fun owning these balls, and soon enough they'll grow tired, roll under the cupboard, and be quiet. Despite this deliberation, however, Blumfeld, near to anger, flings the ball to the ground, and it is a miracle that in doing so the delicate, all but transparent celluloid cover doesn't break. Without hesitation the two balls resume their former low, well-co-ordinated jumps.

Blumfeld undresses calmly, arranges his clothes in the wardrobe which he always inspects carefully to make sure the charwoman has left everything in order. Once or twice he glances over his shoulder at the balls, which, unpursued, seem to be pursuing him; they have followed him and are now jumping close behind him. Blumfeld puts on his dressing gown and sets out for the opposite wall to fetch one of the pipes which are hanging in a rack. Before turning round he instinctively kicks his foot out backwards, but the balls know how to get out of its way and remain untouched. As Blumfeld goes off to fetch the pipe the balls at once follow close behind him; he shuffles along in his slippers, taking irregular steps, yet each step is followed almost without pause by the sound of the balls; they are keeping pace with him. To see how the balls manage to do this, Blumfeld turns suddenly round. But hardly has he turned when the balls describe a semicircle and are already behind him again, and this they repeat every time he turns. Like submissive companions, they try to avoid appearing in front of Blumfeld. Up to the present they have evidently dared to do so only in order to introduce themselves; now, however, it seems they have actually entered into his service.

Hitherto, when faced with situations he couldn't master, Blumfeld had always chosen to behave as though he hadn't noticed any-

thing. It had often helped and usually im-
proved the situation. This, then, is what he
does now; he takes up a position in front of
the pipe rack and, puffing out his lips, chooses
a pipe, fills it with particular care from the
tobacco pouch close at hand, and allows the
balls to continue their jumping behind him.
But he hesitates to approach the table, for
to hear the sound of the jumps coinciding
with that of his own steps almost hurts him.
So there he stands, and while taking an un-
necessarily long time to fill his pipe he measures the distance separating him from the
table. At last, however, he overcomes his faint-
heartedness and covers the distance with such
stamping of feet that he cannot hear the balls.
But the moment he is seated he can hear
them jumping up and down behind his chair
as distinctly as ever.

Above the table, within reach, a shelf is
nailed to the wall on which stands the bottle
of kirsch surrounded by little glasses. Beside
it, in a pile, lie several copies of the French
magazine. (This very day the latest issue has
arrived and Blumfeld takes it down. He quite

forgets the kirsch; he even has the feeling that today he is proceeding with his usual activities only to console himself, for he feels no genuine desire to read. Contrary to his usual habit of carefully turning one page after the other, he opens the magazine at random and there finds a large photograph. He forces himself to examine it in detail. It shows a meeting between the Czar of Russia and the President of France. This takes place on a ship. All about as far as can be seen are many other ships, the smoke from their funnels vanishing in the bright sky. Both Czar and President have rushed towards each other with long strides and are clasping one another by the hand. Behind the Czar as well as behind the President stand two men. By comparison with the gay faces of the Czar and the President, the faces of their attendants are very solemn, the eyes of each group focused on their master. Lower down—the scene evidently takes place on the top deck—stand long lines of saluting sailors cut off by the margin. Gradually Blumfeld contemplates the picture with more interest, then holds it a little further away and looks at it with blinking eyes. He has always had a taste for such imposing scenes. The way the chief personages clasp each other's hand so naturally, so cordially and lightheartedly, this he finds most lifelike. And it's just as appropriate that the attendants—high-ranking gentlemen, of course, with their names printed beneath—express in their bearing the solemnity of the historical moment.)

And instead of helping himself to everything he needs, Blumfeld sits there tense, staring at the bowl of his still unlit pipe. He is lying in wait. Suddenly, quite unexpectedly, his numbness leaves him and with a jerk he turns round in his chair. But the balls, equally alert, or perhaps automatically following the law governing them, also change their position the moment Blumfeld turns, and hide behind his back. Blumfeld now sits with his back to the table, the cold pipe in his hand. And now the balls jump under the table and, since there's a rug there, they are less audible. This is a great advantage: only faint, hollow noises can be heard, one has to pay great at-

tention to catch their sound. Blumfeld, however, does pay great attention, and hears them
distinctly. But this is so only for the moment,
in a little while he probably won't hear them
any more. The fact that they cannot make
themselves more audible on the rug strikes
Blumfeld as a great weakness on the part of
the balls. What one has to do is lay one or
even better two rugs under them and they are
all but powerless. Admittedly only for a lim-
ited time, and besides, their very existence
wields a certain power.

Right now Blumfeld could have made good
use of a dog, a wild young animal would soon
have dealt with these balls; he imagines this
dog trying to catch them with its paws, chasing them from their positions, hunting them
all over the room, and finally getting hold of
them between its teeth. It's quite possible that
before long Blumfeld will acquire a dog.

For the moment, however, the balls have
no one to fear but Blumfeld, and he has no
desire to destroy them just now, perhaps he
lacks the necessary determination. He comes
home in the evening tired from work and just

when he is in need of some rest he is faced
with this surprise. Only now does he realize
how tired he really is. No doubt he will destroy the balls, and that in the near future,
but not just yet, probably not until tomorrow.
If one looks at the whole thing with an
unprejudiced eye, the balls behave modestly
enough. From time to time, for instance, they
could jump into the foreground, show themselves, and then return again to their positions, or they could jump higher so as to beat
against the tabletop in order to compensate
themselves for the muffling effect of the rug.
But this they don't do, they don't want to ir-
ritate Blumfeld unduly, they are evidently confining themselves to what is absolutely necessary.

Even this measured necessity, however, is
quite sufficient to spoil Blumfeld's rest at the
table. He has been sitting there only a few
minutes and is already considering going to
bed. One of his motives for this is that he
can't smoke here, for he has left the matches
on his bedside table. Thus he would have to
fetch these matches, but once having reached

the bedside table he might as well stay there and lie down. For this he has an ulterior motive: he thinks that the balls, with their mania for keeping behind him, will jump onto the bed, and that there, in lying down, on purpose or not, he will squash them. The objection that what would then remain of the balls could still go on jumping, he dismisses. Even the unusual must have its limits. Complete balls jump anyway, even if not incessantly, but fragments of balls never jump, and consequently will not jump in this case, either. "Up!" he shouts, having grown almost reckless from this reflection and, the balls still behind him, he stamps off to bed. His hope seems to be confirmed, for when he purposely takes up a position quite near the bed, one ball promptly springs onto it. Then, however, the unexpected occurs: the other ball disappears under the bed. The possibility that the balls could jump under the bed as well had not occurred to Blumfeld. He is outraged about the one ball, although he is aware how unjust this is, for by jumping under the bed the ball fulfills its duty perhaps better than the ball on the bed. Now everything depends on which place the balls decide to choose, for Blumfeld does not believe that they can work separately for any length of time. And sure enough a moment later the ball on the floor also jumps onto the bed. Now I've got them, thinks Blumfeld, hot with joy, and tears his dressing gown from his body to throw himself into bed. At that moment, however, the very same ball jumps back under the bed. Overwhelmed with disappointment, Blumfeld almost collapses. Very likely the ball just took a good look round up there and decided it didn't like it. And now the other one has followed, too, and of course remains, for it's better down there. "Now I'll have these drummers with me all night," thinks Blumfeld, biting his lips and nodding his head.

He feels gloomy, without actually knowing what harm the balls could do him in the night. He is a good sleeper, he will easily be able to ignore so slight a noise. To make quite sure of this and mindful of his past experience, he lays two rugs on the floor. It's as if he owned a little dog for which he wants to make a soft bed. And as though the balls had also grown tired and sleepy, their jumping has become lower and slower than before. As Blumfeld kneels beside the bed, lamp in hand, he thinks for a moment that the balls might come to rest on the rug—they fall so weakly, roll so slowly along. Then, however, they dutifully rise again. Yet it is quite possible that in the morning when Blumfeld looks under the bed he'll find there two quiet, harmless children's balls.

But it seems that they may not even be able to keep up their jumping until the morning, for as soon as Blumfeld is in bed he doesn't hear them any more. He strains his ears, leans out of bed to listen—not a sound. The effect of the rugs can't be as strong as that; the only explanation is that the balls are no longer jumping, either because they aren't able to bounce themselves off the rug and have therefore abandoned jumping for the time being or, which is more likely, they will never jump again. Blumfeld could get up and see exactly what's going on, but in his relief at finding peace at last he prefers to remain where he is. He would rather not risk disturbing the pacified balls even with his eyes. Even smoking he happily renounces, turns over on his side, and promptly goes to sleep.

But he does not remain undisturbed; as usual he sleeps without dreaming, but very restlessly. Innumerable times during the night he is startled by the delusion that some-one is knocking at his door. He knows quite well that no one is knocking; who would knock at night and at his lonely bachelor's door? Yet although he knows this for certain, he is startled again and again and each time glances in suspense at the door, his mouth open, eyes wide, a strand of hair trembling over his damp forehead. He tries to count how many times he has been woken but, dizzy from the huge numbers he arrives at, he falls back to sleep again. He thinks he knows where the knocking comes from; not from the door, but somewhere quite different; being heavy with sleep, however, he cannot quite remember on what his suspicions are based. All he knows is that innumerable tiny unpleasant sounds accumulate before producing the great strong knocking. He would happily suffer all the unpleasantness of the small sounds if he could be spared the actual knocking, but for some reason it's too late; he cannot interfere, the moment has passed, he can't even speak, his mouth opens but all that comes out is a silent yawn, and furious at this he thrusts his face into the pillows. Thus the night passes.

In the morning he is awakened by the char-woman's knocking; with a sigh of relief he welcomes the gentle tap on the door whose inaudibility has in the past always been one of his sources of complaint. He is about to shout "Come in!" when he hears another lively, faint, yet all but belligerent knocking. It's the balls under the bed. Have they woken up? Have they, unlike him, gathered new strength over-night? "Just a moment," shouts Blumfeld to the charwoman, jumps out of bed and, taking great care to keep the balls behind him, throws himself on the floor, his back still towards them; then, twisting his head over his shoulder, he glances at the balls and—nearly lets out a curse. Like children pushing away blankets that annoy them at night, the balls have appar-ently spent all night pushing the rugs, with

tiny twitching movements, so far away from
under the bed that they are now once more
on the parquet, where they can continue making their noise. "Back onto the rugs!" says
Blumfeld with an angry face, and only when
the balls, thanks to the rugs, have become
quiet again, does he call in the charwoman.
While she—a fat, dull-witted, stiff-backed
woman—is laying the breakfast on the table
and doing the few necessary chores, Blumfeld
stands motionless in his dressing gown by his
bed so as to keep the balls in their place. With
his eyes he follows the charwoman to see
whether she notices anything. This, since she
is hard of hearing, is very unlikely, and the
fact that Blumfeld thinks he sees the charwoman stopping here and there, holding on to
some furniture and listening with raised eyebrows, he puts down to his overwrought con-
dition caused by a bad night's sleep. It would
relieve him if he could persuade the charwoman to speed up her work, but if anything
she is slower than usual. She loads herself
laboriously with Blumfeld's clothes and shuffles out with them into the corridor, stays away

a long time, and the din she makes beating the clothes echoes in his ears with slow, monotonous thuds. And during all this time Blumfeld has to remain on the bed, cannot move for fear of drawing the balls behind him, has to let the coffee—which he likes to drink as hot as possible—get cold, and can do nothing but stare at the drawn blinds behind which the day is dimly dawning. At last the charwoman has finished, bids him good morning, and is about to leave; but before she actually goes she hesitates by the door, moves her lips a little, and takes a long look at Blumfeld. Blumfeld is about to remonstrate when she at last departs. Blumfeld longs to fling the door open and shout after her that she is a stupid, idiotic old woman. However, when he reflects on what he actually has against her, he can only think of the paradox of her having clearly noticed nothing and yet trying to give the impression that she has. How confused his thoughts have become! And all on account of a bad night. Some explanation for his poor sleep he finds in the fact that last night he deviated from his usual habits by not smoking or drinking any schnapps. When for once I don't smoke or drink schnapps— and this is the result of his reflections—I sleep badly.

From now on he is going to take better care of his health, and he begins by fetching some cotton wool from his medicine chest which hangs over his bedside table and putting two little wads of it into his ears. Then he stands up and takes a trial step. Although the balls do follow he can hardly hear them; the addition of another wad makes them quite inaudible. Blumfeld takes a few more steps; nothing particularly unpleasant happens. Everyone for himself, Blumfeld as well as the balls, and although they are bound to one another they don't disturb each other. Only once, when Blumfeld turns round rather suddenly and one ball fails to make the countermovement fast enough, does he touch it with his knee. But this is the only incident. Otherwise Blumfeld calmly drinks his coffee; he is as hungry as though, instead of sleeping last night, he had gone for a long walk; he washes in cold, exceedingly refreshing water, and puts

on his clothes. He still hasn't pulled up the
blinds; rather, as a precaution, he has preferred to remain in semidarkness; he has no
wish for the balls to be seen by other eyes.
But now that he is ready to go he has somehow to provide for the balls in case they
should dare—not that he thinks they will—to
follow him into the street. He thinks of a good
solution, opens the large wardrobe, and places
himself with his back to it. As though divin-
ing his intention, the balls steer clear of the
wardrobe's interior, taking advantage of every
inch of space between Blumfeld and the
wardrobe; when there's no other alternative
they jump into the wardrobe for a moment,
but when faced by the dark out they promptly
jump again. Rather than be lured over the
edge further into the wardrobe, they neglect
their duty and stay by Blumfeld's side. But
their little ruses avail them nothing, for now
Blumfeld himself climbs backward into the
wardrobe and they have to follow him. And
with this their fate has been sealed, for on the
floor of the wardrobe lie various smallish ob-
jects such as boots, boxes, small trunks which,

although carefully arranged—Blumfeld now
regrets this—nevertheless considerably hamper the balls. And when Blumfeld, having by
now pulled the door almost to, jumps out of it
with an enormous leap such as he has not
made for years, slams the door and turns the
key, the balls are imprisoned. "Well, that
worked," thinks Blumfeld, wiping the sweat
from his face. What a din the balls are making in the wardrobe! It sounds as though they
are desperate. Blumfeld, on the other hand,
is very contented. He leaves the room and
already the deserted corridor has a soothing
effect on him. He takes the wool out of his
ears and is enchanted by the countless sounds
of the waking house. Few people are to be
seen, it's still very early.

Downstairs in the hall in front of the low
door leading to the charwoman's basement
apartment stands that woman's ten-year-
old son. The image of his mother, not one
feature of the woman has been omitted in this
child's face. Bandy-legged, hands in his trouser pockets, he stands there wheezing, for he
already has a goiter and can breathe only

with difficulty. But whereas Blumfeld, whenever the boy crosses his path, usually quickens his step to spare himself the spectacle, today he almost feels like pausing for a moment. Even if the boy has been brought into the world by this woman and shows every sign of his origin, he is nevertheless a child, the thoughts of a child still dwell in this shapeless head, and if one were to speak to him sensibly and ask him something, he would very likely answer in a bright voice, innocent and reverential, and after some inner struggle one could bring oneself to pat these cheeks. Although this is what Blumfeld thinks, he nevertheless passes him by. In the street he realizes that the weather is pleasanter than he had suspected from his room. The morning mist has dispersed and patches of blue sky have appeared, brushed by a strong wind. Blumfeld has the balls to thank for his having left his room much earlier than usual; even the paper he has left unread on the table; in any case he has saved a great deal of time and can now afford to walk slowly. It is remarkable how little he worries about the balls now that he is separated from them. So long as they were following him they could have been considered as something belonging to him, something which, in passing judgment on his person, had somehow to be taken into consideration. Now, however, they were mere toys in his wardrobe at home. And it occurs to Blumfeld that the best way of rendering the balls harmless would be to put them to their original use. There in the hall stands the boy; Blumfeld will give him the balls, not lend them, but actually present them to him, which is surely tantamount to ordering their destruction. And even if they were to remain intact they would mean even less in the boy's hands than in the wardrobe, the whole house would watch the boy playing with them, other children would join in, and the general opinion that the balls are things to play with and in no way life companions of Blumfeld would be firmly and irrefutably established. Blumfeld runs back into the house. The boy has just gone down the basement stairs and is about to open the door. So Blumfeld has to call the boy and pronounce his name, a name that to

him seems as ludicrous as everything else connected with the child. "Alfred! Alfred!" he
shouts. The boy hesitates for a long time.
"Come here!" shouts Blumfeld, "I've got
something for you." The janitor's two little
girls appear from the door opposite and, full of
curiosity, take up positions on either side of
Blumfeld. They grasp the situation much more
quickly than the boy and cannot understand
why he doesn't come at once. Without taking
their eyes off Blumfeld they beckon to the
boy, but cannot fathom what kind of present
is awaiting Alfred. Tortured with curiosity,
they hop from one foot to the other. Blumfeld
laughs at them as well as at the boy. The latter seems to have figured it all out and climbs
stiffly, clumsily up the steps. Not even in his
gait can he manage to belie his mother, who,
incidentally, has appeared in the basement
doorway. To make sure that the charwoman
also understands and in the hope that she will
supervise the carrying out of his instructions,
should it be necessary, Blumfeld shouts exces-
sively loud. "Up in my room," says Blumfeld,
"I have two lovely balls. Would you like to

have them?" Not knowing how to behave, the boy simply screws up his mouth, turns round and looks inquiringly down at his mother. The girls, however, promptly begin to jump around Blumfeld and ask him for the balls. "You will be allowed to play with them too," Blumfeld tells them, but waits for the boy's answer. He could of course give the balls to the girls, but they strike him as too unreliable and for the moment he has more confidence in the boy. Meanwhile, the latter, without having exchanged a word, has taken counsel with his mother and nods his assent to Blumfeld's repeated question. "Then listen," says Blumfeld, who is quite prepared to receive no thanks for his gift. "Your mother has the key of my door, you must borrow it from her. But here is the key of my wardrobe, and in the wardrobe you will find the balls. Take good care to lock the wardrobe and the room again. But with the balls you can do what you like and you don't have to bring them back. Have you understood me?" Unfortunately, the boy has not understood. Blumfeld has tried to make everything particularly clear to this hopelessly dense creature, but for this very reason has repeated everything too often, has in turn too often mentioned keys, room, and wardrobe, and as a result the boy stares at him as though he were rather a seducer than his benefactor. The girls, on the other hand, have understood everything immediately, press against Blumfeld, and stretch out their hands for the key. "Wait a moment," says Blumfeld, by now annoyed with them all. Time, moreover, is passing, he can't stand about much longer. If only the mother would say that she has understood him and take matters in hand for the boy! Instead of which she still stands down by the door, smiles with the affectation of the bashful deaf, and is probably under the impression that Blumfeld up there has suddenly fallen for the boy and is hearing him his lessons. Blumfeld on the other hand can't very well climb down the basement stairs and shout into the charwoman's ear to make her son for God's sake relieve him of the balls! It had required enough of his self-control as it was to entrust the key of his wardrobe for a whole day to this family. It is certainly not

in order to save himself trouble that he is
handing the key to the boy rather than himself leading the boy up and there giving him
the balls. But he can't very well first give the
balls away and then immediately deprive the
boy of them by—as would be bound to happen—drawing them after him as his followers.
"So you still don't understand me?" asks
Blumfeld almost wistfully after having started a
fresh explanation which, however, he immediately interrupts at sight of the boy's vacant
stare. So vacant a stare renders one helpless.
It could tempt one into saying more than one
intends, if only to fill the vacancy with sense.
Whereupon "We'll fetch the balls for him!"
shout the girls. They are shrewd and have
realized that they can obtain the balls only
through using the boy as an intermediary, but
that they themselves have to bring about this
mediation. From the janitor's room a clock
strikes, warning Blumfeld to hurry. "Well,
then, take the key," says Blumfeld, and the
key is more snatched from his hand than given
by him. He would have handed it to the boy
with infinitely more confidence. "The key to

the room you'll have to get from the woman,"
Blumfeld adds. "And when you return with
the balls you must hand both keys to her."
"Yes, yes!" shout the girls and run down the
steps. They know everything, absolutely everything; and as though Blumfeld were in-
fected by the boy's denseness, he is unable to
understand how they could have grasped everything so quickly from his explanations.

Now they are already tugging at the charwoman's skirt but, tempting as it would be,
Blumfeld cannot afford to watch them carrying out their task, not only because it's already
late, but also because he has no desire to be
present at the liberation of the balls. He would
in fact far prefer to be several streets away
when the girls first open the door of his room.
After all, how does he know what else he
might have to expect from these balls! And so
for the second time this morning he leaves the
house. He has one last glimpse of the charwoman defending herself against the girls,
and of the boy stirring his bandy legs to come
to his mother's assistance. It's beyond Blumfeld's comprehension why a creature like this

servant should prosper and propagate in this world.

While on his way to the linen factory, where Blumfeld is employed, thoughts about his work gradually get the upper hand. He quickens his step and, despite the delay caused by the boy, he is the first to arrive in his office. This office is a glass-enclosed room containing a writing desk for Blumfeld and two standing desks for the two assistants subordinate to him. Although these standing desks are so small and narrow as to suggest they are meant for school children, this office is very crowded and the assistants cannot sit down, for then there would be no place for Blumfeld's chair. As a result they stand all day, pressed against their desks. For them of course this is very uncomfortable, but it also makes it very difficult for Blumfeld to keep an eye on them. They often press eagerly against their desks not so much in order to work as to whisper to one another or even to take forty winks. They give Blumfeld a great deal of trouble; they don't help him sufficiently with the enormous amount of work that is imposed on him. This

work involves supervising the whole distribution of fabrics and cash among the women
homeworkers who are employed by the factory for the manufacture of certain fancy
commodities. To appreciate the magnitude of
this task an intimate knowledge of the general
conditions is necessary. But since Blumfeld's
immediate superior has died some years ago,
no one any longer possesses this knowledge,
which is also why Blumfeld cannot grant anyone the right to pronounce an opinion on his
work. The manufacturer, Herr Ottomar, for
instance, clearly underestimates Blumfeld's
work; no doubt he recognizes that in the
course of twenty years Blumfeld has deserved
well of the factory, and this he acknowledges
not only because he is obliged to, but also because he respects Blumfeld as a loyal, trustworthy person.—He underestimates his work,
nevertheless, for he believes it could be con-
ducted by methods more simple and therefore
in every respect more profitable than those employed by Blumfeld. It is said, and it is probably not incorrect, that Ottomar shows himself
so rarely in Blumfeld's department simply to

spare himself the annoyance which the sight of Blumfeld's working methods causes him. To be so unappreciated is undoubtedly sad for Blumfeld, but there is no remedy, for he cannot very well compel Ottomar to spend let us say a whole month on end in Blumfeld's department in order to study the great variety of work being accomplished there, to apply his own allegedly better methods, and to let himself be convinced of Blumfeld's soundness by the collapse of the department—which would be the inevitable result. And so Blumfeld carries on his work undeterred as before, gives a little start whenever Ottomar appears after a long absence, then with the subordinate's sense of duty makes a feeble effort to explain to Ottomar this or that arrangement, whereupon the latter, his eyes lowered and giving a silent nod, passes on. But what worries Blumfeld more than this lack of appreciation is the thought that one day he will be compelled to leave his job, the immediate consequence of which will be pandemonium, a confusion no one will be able to straighten out because so far as he knows there isn't a single soul in the factory capable of replacing him and of carrying on his job in a manner that could be relied upon to prevent months of the most serious interruptions. Needless to say, if the boss underestimates an employee the latter's colleagues try their best to surpass him in this respect. In consequence everyone underestimates Blumfeld's work; no one considers it necessary to spend any time training in Blumfeld's department, and when new employees are hired not one of them is ever assigned to Blumfeld. As a result Blumfeld's department lacks a younger generation to carry on. When Blumfeld, who up to then had been managing the entire department with the help of only one servant, demanded an assistant, weeks of bitter fighting ensued. Almost every day Blumfeld appeared in Ottomar's office and explained to him calmly and in minute detail why an assistant was needed in his department. He was needed not by any means because Blumfeld wished to spare himself, Blumfeld had no intention of sparing himself, he was doing more than his share of work and this he had no desire to change, but would Herr Ottomar please consider how in the course of time the business had grown, how every department had been correspondingly enlarged, with the exception of Blumfeld's department, which was invariably forgotten! And would he consider too how the work had increased just there! When Blumfeld had entered the firm, a time Herr Ottomar probably could not remember, they had employed some ten seamstresses, today the number varied between fifty and sixty. Such a job requires great energy; Blumfeld could guarantee that he was completely wearing himself out in this work, but that he will continue to master it completely he can henceforth no longer guarantee. True, Herr Ottomar had never flatly refused Blumfeld's requests, this was something he could not do to an old employee, but the manner in which he hardly listened, in which he talked to others over Blumfeld's head, made halfhearted promises and had forgotten everything in a few days—this behavior was insulting to say the least. Not actually to Blumfeld, Blumfeld is no romantic, pleasant as honor and recognition may be, Blumfeld can do without them, in spite of everything he will stick to his desk as long as it is at all possible, in any case he is in the right, and right, even though on occasion it may take a long time, must prevail in the end. True, Blumfeld has at last been given two assistants, but what assistants! One might have thought Ottomar had realized he could express his contempt for the department even better by granting rather than by refusing it these assistants. It was even possible that Ottomar had kept Blumfeld waiting so long because he was looking for two assistants just like these, and—as may be imagined—took a long time to find them. And now of course Blumfeld could no longer complain; if he did, the answer could easily be foreseen: after all, he had asked for one assistant and had been given two, that's how cleverly Ottomar had arranged things. Needless to say, Blumfeld complained just the same, but only because his predicament all but forced him to do so, not because he still hoped for any redress. Nor did he complain emphatically, but only by the way, whenever the occasion arose. Nevertheless, among his spiteful colleagues the rumor soon spread that someone had asked Ottomar if it were really possible that Blumfeld, who after all had been given such unusual aid, was still complaining. To which Ottomar answered that this was correct, Blumfeld was still complaining, and rightly so. He, Ottomar, had at last realized this and he intended gradually to assign to Blumfeld one assistant for each seamstress, in other words some sixty in all. In case this number should prove insufficient, however, he would let him have even more and would not cease until the bedlam, which had been developing for years in Blumfeld's department, was complete. Now it cannot be denied that in this remark Ottomar's manner of speech had been cleverly imitated, but Blumfeld had no doubts whatever that Ottomar would not dream of speaking about him in such a way. The whole thing was a fabrication of the loafers in the offices on the first floor. Blumfeld ignored it—if only he could as calmly have ignored the presence of the assistants! But there they stood, and could not be spirited away. Pale, weak children. According to their

credentials they had already passed school
age, but in reality this was difficult to believe.
In fact their rightful place was so clearly at
their mother's knee that one would hardly
have dared to entrust them to a teacher. They
still couldn't even move properly; standing up
for any length of time tired them inordinately,
especially when they first arrived. When left
to themselves they promptly doubled up in
their weakness, standing hunched and
crooked in their corner. Blumfeld tried to point
out to them that if they went on giving in to
their indolence they would become cripples
for life. To ask the assistants to make the
slightest move was to take a risk; once when
one of them had been ordered to carry something a short distance, he had run so eagerly
that he had banged his knee against a desk.
The room had been full of seamstresses, the
desks covered in merchandise, but Blumfeld
had been obliged to neglect everything and take
the sobbing assistant into the office and there
bandage his wound. Yet even this zeal on the
part of the assistant was superficial; like actual children they tried once in a while to ex-

cel, but far more often—indeed almost always —they tried to divert their superior's attention and to cheat him. Once, at a time of the most intensive work, Blumfeld had rushed past them, dripping with sweat, and had observed them secretly swapping stamps among the bales of merchandise. He had felt like banging them on the head with his fists, it would have been the only possible punishment for such behavior, but they were after all only children and Blumfeld could not very well knock children down. And so he continued to put up with them. Originally he had imagined that the assistants would help him with the essential chores which at the moment of the distribution of goods required so much effort and vigilance. He had imagined himself standing in the center behind his desk, keeping an eye on everything and making the entries in the books while the assistants ran to and fro, distributing everything according to his orders. He had imagined that his supervision, which, sharp as it was, could not cope with such a crowd, would be complemented by the assistants' attention; he had hoped that

these assistants would gradually acquire experience, cease depending entirely on his orders, and finally learn to discriminate on their
own between the seamstresses as to their trust-
worthiness and requirements. Blumfeld soon
realized that all these hopes had been in vain
and that he could not afford to let them even
talk to the seamstresses. From the beginning
they had ignored some of the seamstresses,
either from fear or dislike; others to whom
they felt partial they would sometimes run to
meet at the door. To them the assistants
would bring whatever the women wanted,
pressing it almost secretly into their hands, although the seamstresses were perfectly entitled to receive it, would collect on a bare
shelf for these favorites various cuttings,
worthless remnants, but also a few still useful
odds and ends, waving them blissfully at the
women behind Blumfeld's back and in return having sweets popped into their mouths.
Blumfeld of course soon put an end to this
mischief and the moment the seamstresses arrived he ordered the assistants back into their
glass-enclosed cubicles. But for a long time

they considered this to be a grave injustice, they sulked, willfully broke their nibs, and sometimes, although not daring to raise their heads, even knocked loudly against the glass panes in order to attract the seamstresses' attention to the bad treatment which in their opinion they were suffering at Blumfeld's hands.

The wrong they do themselves the assistants cannot see. For instance, they almost always arrive late at the office. Blumfeld, their superior, who from his earliest youth has considered it natural to arrive half an hour before the office opens—not from ambition or an exaggerated sense of duty but simply from a certain feeling of decency—often has to wait more than an hour for his assistants. Chewing his breakfast roll he stands behind his desk, looking through the accounts in the seamstresses' little books. Soon he is immersed in his work and thinking of nothing else when suddenly he receives such a shock that his pen continues to tremble in his hand for some while afterwards. One of the assistants has dashed in, looking as though he is about to collapse; he is holding on to something with one hand while the other is pressed against his heaving chest. All this, however, simply means that he is making excuses for being late, excuses so absurd that Blumfeld purposely ignores them, for if he didn't he would have to give the young man a well-deserved thrashing. As it is, he just glances at him for a moment, points with outstretched hand at the cubicle, and turns back to his work. Now one really might expect the assistant to appreciate his superior's kindness and hurry to his place. No, he doesn't hurry, he dawdles about, he walks on tiptoe, slowly placing one foot in front of the other. Is he trying to ridicule his superior? No. Again it's just that mixture of fear and self-complacency against which one is powerless. How else explain the fact that even today Blumfeld, who has himself arrived unusually late in the office and now after a long wait— he doesn't feel like checking the books—sees, through the clouds of dust raised by the stupid servant with his broom, the two assistants sauntering peacefully along the street? Arm in arm, they appear to be telling one another important things which, however, are sure to have only the remotest and very likely irreverent connections with the office. The nearer they approach the glass door, the slower they walk. One of them seizes the door handle but fails to turn it; they just go on talking, listening, laughing. "Hurry out and open the door for our gentlemen!" shouts Blumfeld at the servant, throwing up his hands. But when the assistants come in, Blumfeld no longer feels like quarrelling, ignores their greetings, and goes to his desk. He starts doing his accounts, but now and again glances up to see what his assistants are up to. One of them seems to be very tired and rubs his eyes. When hanging up his overcoat he takes the opportunity to lean against the wall. On the street he seemed lively enough, but the proximity of work tires him. The other assistant, however, is eager to work, but only work of a certain kind. For a long time it has been his wish to be allowed to sweep. But this is work to which he is not entitled; sweeping is exclusively the servant's job; in itself Blumfeld would have nothing against the assistant sweeping, let the assistant sweep, he can't make a worse job of it than the servant, but if the assistant wants to sweep then he must come earlier, before the servant begins to sweep, and not spend on it time that is reserved exclusively for office work. But since the young man is totally deaf to any sensible argument, at least the servant—that half-blind old buffer whom the boss would certainly not tolerate in any department but Blumfeld's and who is still alive only by the grace of the boss and God—at least the servant might be sensible and hand the broom for a moment to the young man who, being clumsy, would soon lose his interest and run after the servant with the broom in order to persuade him to go on sweeping. It appears, however, that the servant feels especially responsible for the sweeping; one can see how he, the moment the young man approaches him, tries to grasp the broom more firmly with his trembling hands; he even stands still and stops sweeping so as to direct his full attention to the ownership of the broom. The assistant doesn't actually plead in words, for he is afraid of Blumfeld, who is ostensibly doing his accounts;

moreover, ordinary speech is useless, since the servant can be made to hear only by excessive shouting. So at first the assistant tugs the servant by the sleeve. The servant knows, of course, what it is about, glowers at the assistant, shakes his head and pulls the broom nearer, up to his chest. Whereupon the assistant folds his hands and pleads. Actually, he has no hope of achieving anything by pleading, but the pleading amuses him and so he pleads. The other assistant follows the goings-on with low laughter and seems to think, heaven knows why, that Blumfeld can't hear him. The pleading makes not the slightest impression on the servant, who turns round and thinks he can safely use the broom again. The assistant, however, has skipped after him on tiptoe and, rubbing his hands together imploringly, now pleads from another side. This turning of the one and skipping of the other is repeated several times. Finally the servant feels cut off from all sides and realizes—something which, had he been slightly less stupid, he might have realized from the beginning— that he will be tired out long before the assistant. So, looking for help elsewhere, he wags his finger at the assistant and points at Blumfeld, suggesting that he will lodge a complaint if the assistant refuses to desist. The assistant realizes that if he is to get the broom at all he'll have to hurry, so he impudently makes a grab for it. An involuntary scream from the other assistant heralds the imminent decision. The servant saves the broom once more by taking a step back and dragging it after him. But now the assistant is up in arms: with open mouth and flashing eyes he leaps forward, the servant tries to escape, but his old legs wobble rather than run, the assistant tugs at the broom and though he doesn't succeed in getting it he nevertheless causes it to drop and in this way it is lost to the servant. Also apparently to the assistant for, the moment the broom falls, all three, the two assistants and the servant, are paralyzed, for now Blumfeld is bound to discover everything. And sure enough Blumfeld at his peephole glances up as though taking in the situation only now. He stares at each one with a stern and searching eye, even the broom on the floor does not escape his notice. Perhaps the silence has lasted too long or perhaps the assistant can no longer suppress his desire to sweep, in any case he bends down—albeit very carefully, as though about to grab an animal rather than a broom —seizes it, passes it over the floor, but, when Blumfeld jumps up and steps out of his cubicle, promptly casts it aside in alarm. "Both of you back to work! And not another sound out of you!" shouts Blumfeld, and with an out-stretched hand he directs the two assistants back to their desks. They obey at once, but not shamefaced or with lowered heads, rather they squeeze themselves stiffly past Blumfeld, staring him straight in the eye as though try-ing in this way to stop him from beating them. Yet they might have learned from experience that Blumfeld on principle never beats any-one. But they are overapprehensive, and with-out any tact keep trying to protect their real or imaginary rights.

THE WARDEN
OF THE TOMB

Small workroom, high window, beyond it a bare treetop. PRINCE (*at writing table, leaning back in chair, looking out of window*). CHAMBERLAIN (*white beard, youthfully squeezed into tight jacket, standing against wall near center door*).

Pause.

P R I N C E (*turning from window*): Well?

C H A M B E R L A I N : I cannot recommend it, your Highness.

P R I N C E : Why?

C H A M B E R L A I N : I can't quite formulate my objections at the moment. I'm expressing only a fraction of what's on my mind when I quote the universal saying: Let the dead rest in peace.

P R I N C E : That's my opinion, too.

C H A M B E R L A I N : In that case I haven't properly understood.

P R I N C E : So it seems.

Pause.

P R I N C E : Perhaps the only thing that disconcerts you is that instead of going ahead with the arrangement, I announced it to you first.

C H A M B E R L A I N : The announcement certainly burdens me with a great responsibility which I must endeavor to live up to.

P R I N C E : Don't speak of responsibility! *Pause.*

P R I N C E : Let's see. Hitherto the tomb in the Friedrichspark has been guarded by a warden who lives in a lodge at the park's entrance. Was there anything wrong with this?

C H A M B E R L A I N : Certainly not. The tomb is more than four hundred years old and has always been guarded in this way.

P R I N C E : It could be an abuse. But it isn't an abuse, is it?

C H A M B E R L A I N : It is a necessary arrangement.

P R I N C E : All right then, a necessary arrangement. I've been here in the castle

150

quite some time now, have gained some insight into details which hitherto have been entrusted to strangers—they manage fairly well—and I've come to this conclusion: the Warden up there in the park is not enough. There must also be a guard down in the tomb. It probably won't be a pleasant job. But experience has proved that willing and suitable people can be found for any job.

CHAMBERLAIN: Needless to say, any orders issued by your Highness will be carried out, even if the necessity of the order is not fully understood.

PRINCE (*starting up*): Necessity! Do you mean to say that a guard at the park gate is necessary? The Friedrichspark belongs to the castle park, is entirely surrounded by it. The castle park itself is amply guarded—by the army, what's more. So why a special guard for the Friedrichspark? Isn't this a mere formality? A pleasant deathbed for the wretched old man who is keeping watch there?

C H A M B E R L A I N : Formality it is, but a necessary one. A demonstration of reverence for the illustrious dead.

P R I N C E : And what about the guard in the tomb itself?

C H A M B E R L A I N : In my opinion this would have a police connotation. It would mean a real guarding of unreal things beyond the human sphere.

P R I N C E : For my family this tomb represents the frontier between the Human and the Other, and it's on this frontier that I wish to post a guard. As for the police connotation, as you call it, we can question the Warden himself. I've sent for him. (*Rings a bell.*)

C H A M B E R L A I N : He's a confused old man, if I may say so, already quite out of hand.

P R I N C E : If that's so, all the more reason for strengthening the guard in the way I've suggested.

(*Enter servant.*)

P R I N C E : The Warden of the tomb!

(*Servant leads in Warden, holding him tight round the waist to prevent him from collapsing. Ancient red livery hanging loosely about Warden, brightly polished silver buttons, several decorations. Cap in hand, he trembles under the gentlemen's gaze.*)

P R I N C E : Put him on the divan!

(*Servant lays him down and goes off. Pause. A faint rattling in Warden's throat.*)

P R I N C E (*again in armchair*): Can you hear?

W A R D E N (*tries to answer but fails, is too exhausted, sinks back again*).

P R I N C E : Try to pull yourself together. We're waiting.

C H A M B E R L A I N (*leaning over Prince*): What could this man give information about? And credible and important information at that? He ought to be taken straight to bed.

W A R D E N : Not to bed—still strong—fairly —can still hold my end up.

P R I N C E : So you should. You've only just
turned sixty. Granted, you look very
weak.

W A R D E N : I'll pick up in no time—feel
better in a minute.

P R I N C E : It wasn't meant as a reproach.
I'm only sorry you aren't feeling
well. Have you anything to complain
about?

W A R D E N : Hard work—hard work—not
complaining—but very weak—wrestling
bouts every night.

P R I N C E : What d'you say?

W A R D E N : Hard work.

P R I N C E : You said something else.

W A R D E N : Wrestling bouts.

P R I N C E : Wrestling bouts? What kind of
wrestling bouts?

W A R D E N : With the blessed ancestors.

P R I N C E : I don't understand. D'you have
bad dreams?

W A R D E N : No dreams—don't sleep.

P R I N C E : Then let's hear about these—
these wrestling bouts.

W A R D E N (*remains silent*).

PRINCE (*to Chamberlain*): Why doesn't he speak?

CHAMBERLAIN (*hurrying to Warden*): He may die any minute.

PRINCE (*stands up*).

WARDEN (*as Chamberlain touches him*): Don't, don't, don't! (*Fights off Chamberlain's hands, then collapses in tears.*)

PRINCE: We're tormenting him.

CHAMBERLAIN: How?

PRINCE: I don't know.

CHAMBERLAIN: Coming to the castle, having to present himself here, the sight of your Highness, this questioning—he no longer has the wits to face all this.

PRINCE (*still staring at the Warden*): That's not it. (*Goes to divan, bends over Warden, takes his little skull in his hands.*) Mustn't cry. What are you crying for? We wish you well. I realize your job isn't easy. You've certainly deserved well of my family. So stop crying and tell us all about it.

WARDEN: But I'm so afraid of that gentleman there—— (*Looks at Chamber-*

lain, more threateningly than afraid.)

P R I N C E (*to Chamberlain*): If we want him
to talk I'm afraid you'll have to leave.

C H A M B E R L A I N : But look, your Highness, he's foaming at the mouth. He's seriously ill.

P R I N C E (*absent-mindedly*): Please go, it
won't take long.

Exit Chamberlain.

Prince sits on edge of divan.

Pause.

P R I N C E : Why were you afraid of him?

W A R D E N (*surprisingly composed*): I wasn't
afraid. Me afraid of a servant?

P R I N C E : He's not a servant. He's a Count,
free and rich.

W A R D E N : A servant all the same, you are
the master.

P R I N C E : If you like it that way. But you
said yourself that you were afraid of him.

W A R D E N : I didn't want to say things in
front of him which are meant only for
you. Haven't I already said too much in
front of him?

156

P R I N C E : So we're on terms of intimacy, and yet today is the first time I've seen you.

W A R D E N : Seen for the first time, but you've always known that I (*raising his forefinger*) hold the most important position at Court. You even acknowledged it publicly by awarding me the medal "Red-as-Fire." Here! (*Holds up the medal on his coat.*)

P R I N C E : No, that's the medal for twenty-five years' service at Court. My grandfather gave you that. But I'll decorate you, too.

W A R D E N : Do as you please and grant me whatever you think I deserve. I've acted as your tomb Warden for thirty years.

P R I N C E : Not mine. My reign has lasted hardly a year.

W A R D E N (*lost in thought*): Thirty years. *Pause.*

W A R D E N (*remembering only half of the Prince's remark*): Nights last years there.

157

PRINCE: I haven't yet had a report from your office. What's your work like?

WARDEN: Every night the same. Every night till the heart beats as if it were about to burst.

PRINCE: Is it only night duty, then? Night duty for an old man like you?

WARDEN: That's just it, your Highness. It's day duty. A loafer's job. There one sits, at the front door, with one's mouth open in the sunshine. Sometimes the watchdog pats one on the knee with its paws, and then lies down again. That's all that ever happens.

PRINCE: Well?

WARDEN (*nodding*): But it has been changed to night duty.

PRINCE: By whom?

WARDEN: By the lords of the tomb.

PRINCE: You know them?

WARDEN: Yes.

PRINCE: They come to see you?

WARDEN: Yes.

PRINCE: Last night, too?

WARDEN: Last night, too.

PRINCE : What was it like?

WARDEN (*sitting up straight*): Same as usual.

Prince stands up.

WARDEN : Same as usual. Quiet till midnight. I'm lying in bed—excuse me—smoking my pipe. My granddaughter is asleep in the next bed. At midnight comes the first knock at the window. I look at the clock. Always to the minute. Two more knocks, they mingle with the striking of the tower clock, but I can still hear them. These are no human knuckles. But I know all that and don't budge. Then it clears its throat outside, it's surprised that in spite of all that knocking I haven't opened the window. Let his princely Highness be surprised! The old Warden is still there! (*Shows his fist.*)

PRINCE : You're threatening me?

WARDEN (*doesn't immediately understand*): Not you. The one at the window!

PRINCE: Who is it?

WARDEN: He shows himself at once. All of a sudden window and shutters are opened.

I just have time to throw the blanket over my grandchild's face. The storm blows in, promptly puts the light out. Duke Friedrich! His face with beard and hair completely fills my poor window. How he has grown throughout the centuries! When he opens his mouth to speak the wind blows his old beard between his teeth and he bites on it.

P R I N C E : Just a moment. You say Duke Friedrich? Which Friedrich?

W A R D E N : Duke Friedrich, just Duke Friedrich.

P R I N C E : Is that the name he gives?

W A R D E N (*anxiously*): No, he doesn't give it.

P R I N C E : And yet you know—(*breaking off*)—Go on!

W A R D E N : Shall I go on?

P R I N C E : Of course. All this very much concerns me. There must be an error in the distribution of labor. You're overworked.

W A R D E N (*kneeling*): Don't take my job away, your Highness. Having lived for you all these years, let me also die for you! Don't wall up the grave I'm struggling towards. I serve willingly and am still strong enough to serve. To be granted an audience like today's, to take a rest with my master—this gives me strength for ten years.

PRINCE (*putting Warden back on divan*): No one's going to take your job from you. How could I get along without your experience? But I'll appoint another Warden, then you'll become Head Warden.

WARDEN: Am I not good enough? Have I ever let anyone pass?

PRINCE: Into the Friedrichspark?

WARDEN: No, out of the park. Who'd want to come in? If ever anyone stops at the railing I beckon to him from the window and he runs away. But out! Everyone wants to get out. After midnight you can see all the voices from the grave assembled round my house. I think it's only because they are so closely packed together that the whole lot of them don't burst through my narrow window. If it

gets too bad, however, I grab the lantern
from under my bed, swing it high, and
with laughter and moaning these incredi-
ble creatures scatter in all directions.
Then I can hear them rustling even in
the furthest bush at the end of the park.
But they soon gather together again.

P R I N C E : And do they tell you what they
want?

W A R D E N : First they give orders. Especially Duke Friedrich. No living being
could be so confident. Every night for
thirty years he has been expecting me to
give in.

P R I N C E : If he has been coming for thirty
years it can't be Duke Friedrich, for he
has been dead only fifteen years. On the
other hand, he is the only one of that
name in the tomb.

W A R D E N (*too carried away by his story*):
That I don't know, your Highness, I
never went to school. I only know how he
begins. "Old dog," he begins at the window, "the gentlemen are knocking and
you just stay in your filthy bed." They

162

have a particular grudge against beds, by the way. And now every night we have the same conversation, he outside, I opposite him, my back to the door. I say: "I'm only on day duty." The Duke turns and shouts into the park: "He's only on day duty." Whereupon all the assembled aristocracy burst out laughing. Then the Duke says to me again: "But it is day." I say curtly: "You're wrong." The Duke: "Night or day, open the door." I: "That's against my orders." And with my pipe I point at a notice on the door. The Duke: "But you're our Warden." I: "Your Warden, but employed by the reigning Prince." He: "Our Warden, that's the main thing. So open up, and be quick about it." I: "No." He: "Idiot, you'll lose your job. Prince Leo has invited us for today."

PRINCE (*quickly*): I?

WARDEN: You.

Pause.

WARDEN: When I hear your name I lose my firmness. That's why I have always taken care to lean against the door which is almost the only thing that holds me up. Outside, everyone's singing your name. "Where's the invitation?" I ask weakly. "Bedbug!" he shouts, "you doubt my ducal word?" I say: "I have no orders, so I won't open, I won't open, I won't open!"—"He won't open!" shouts the Duke outside. "So come on, all of you, the whole dynasty! At the door! We'll open it ourselves." And a moment later there's nothing under my window.

Pause.

P R I N C E : Is that all?

W A R D E N : All? My real service begins only now. I rush out of the door, round the house, and promptly run into the Duke and there we are, locked in combat. He so big, I so small, he so broad, I so thin, I can fight only with his feet, but now and again he lifts me up in the air and then I fight up there, too. All his comrades stand round in a circle and make fun of me. One, for instance, cuts open

164

my trousers behind and they all play with the tail of my shirt while I'm fighting. Can't understand why they laugh, as until now I've always won.

PRINCE: How is it possible for you to win? Have you any weapons?

WARDEN: I carried weapons only during the first years. What good could they be against him? They only hampered me. We just fight with our fists, or rather with the strength of our breath. And you're in my thoughts all the time.

Pause.

WARDEN: But I never doubt my victory. Only sometimes I'm afraid the Duke will let me slip through his fingers and forget that he's fighting.

PRINCE: And when do you win?

WARDEN: At dawn. Then he throws me down and spits at me. That's his confession of defeat. But I have to go on lying there for an hour before I can get my breath back properly.

Pause.

P R I N C E (*standing up*) : But tell me, don't you know what they really want?

W A R D E N : To get out of the park.

P R I N C E : But why?

W A R D E N : That I don't know.

P R I N C E : Haven't you asked?

W A R D E N : No.

P R I N C E : Why not?

W A R D E N : It would embarrass me. But if you wish, I'll ask them today.

P R I N C E (*shocked, loud*) : Today!

W A R D E N (*knowingly*) : Yes, today.

P R I N C E : And you can't even guess what they want?

W A R D E N (*thoughtfully*) : No.

Pause.

W A R D E N : Perhaps I ought to add that sometimes in the early mornings while I'm lying there trying to get my breath and even too weak to open my eyes, there comes a delicate, moist creature, rather hairy to the touch, a late-comer, the Countess Isabella. She runs her hand all over me, catches hold of my beard, her whole body glides along my neck, under my chin, and she's in the habit of saying: "Not the others, but me—let me out." I shake my head as much as I can. "I want to go to Prince Leo, to offer him my hand." I keep on shaking my head. "But me, me!" I can still hear her crying, then she's gone. And my granddaughter appears with blankets, wraps me up in them, and waits with me till I can walk on my own. An exceptionally good girl.

P R I N C E : Isabella? The name's unknown to me.

Pause.

P R I N C E : To offer me her hand! (*Goes to window, looks out.*)

Enter servant through center door.

S E R V A N T : Her Highness, m'lady the Princess, awaits you.

P R I N C E (*looks absent-mindedly at servant. Turns to Warden*): Wait till I come back. (*Exit left.*)

Chamberlain enters at once through center door, then the Lord High Steward (youngish man in officer's uniform) through door on right.

WARDEN (*ducks behind divan and flourishes his hands as though seeing ghosts*).

STEWARD: The Prince has gone?

CHAMBERLAIN: Following your advice, the Princess sent for him.

STEWARD: Good. (*Turns suddenly, bends over behind divan.*) And you, miserable ghost, you actually dare to appear here in the princely castle! Aren't you afraid of the great boot that'll kick you through the door?

WARDEN: I'm—I'm——

STEWARD: Quiet, first of all keep quiet, don't utter—and sit down here in this corner! (*To Chamberlain*) I thank you for informing me about the latest princely whim.

CHAMBERLAIN: You inquired about it.

STEWARD: Even so. And now a confidential word. Purposely in front of that creature there. You, Count, are flirting with the opposition.

CHAMBERLAIN: Is that an accusation?

STEWARD: An apprehension, so far.

CHAMBERLAIN : In that case I can answer. I'm not flirting with the opposition, for I don't know it. I can feel the currents, but I steer clear of them. I still represent the open policy that prevailed under Duke Friedrich. At that time the only policy at Court was to serve the Prince. This was made easier by his being a bachelor, but it should never be difficult.

STEWARD : Very sensible—except that one's own nose, however reliable, never points the right way all the time. This can only be achieved by reason. But reason must make decisions. Let's assume the Prince is on the wrong track: does one serve him better by following him down or, with all due respect, by chasing him back? Undoubtedly by chasing him back.

CHAMBERLAIN : You came here with the Princess from a foreign Court, have spent a mere six months here, and you already think you can tell the difference between good and evil in the complicated conditions of this Court?

169

S T E W A R D : He who blinks sees only com-
plications. He who keeps his eyes open
sees the eternal truth in the first hours as
clearly as after a hundred years. Admittedly, in this case, a sad truth which in
the next few days, however, may take a
decisive turn for the better.

C H A M B E R L A I N : I cannot believe that
the decision which you wish to bring
about and which I know only from your
announcement will be a good one. I'm
afraid you misunderstand our Prince, the
Court, and everything here.

S T E W A R D : Whether understood or mis-
understood, the present situation is unbearable.

C H A M B E R L A I N : Unbearable it may be,
but it is founded on the nature of things
as they are here, and we are prepared to
bear it to the end.

S T E W A R D : But not the Princess, not I,
not those who are on our side.

C H A M B E R L A I N : What do you find so
unbearable?

S T E W A R D : Just because the decision is imminent I want to speak frankly. The Prince has a dual nature. The one, concerning itself with government, wavers absent-mindedly in public, disregarding its own privileges. The other nature admittedly searches very painstakingly for a strengthening of its foundations. It searches for them in the past, delving deeper and deeper. What a misunderstanding of the situation! A misunderstanding which doesn't lack greatness— although its defectiveness is even greater than its appearance. Can you fail to see that?

C H A M B E R L A I N : It's not the description I object to, it's the interpretation.

S T E W A R D : The interpretation? And to think that in the hope of getting you to agree, I have judged the situation with more leniency than I actually feel! And I'm still withholding my verdict in order to spare you. But just one thing: in reality the Prince does not need a strengthening of his foundations. If he uses all the power at present at his disposal, he'll find it sufficient to bring about everything that the most extreme responsibility before God and man may demand of him. But he shies away from the balance of life, he's on his way to becoming a tyrant.

CHAMBERLAIN: He with his modest character!

STEWARD: It's the modesty of the one half, for he needs all his energy for the second half which scrapes together the foundation needed to build something like the Tower of Babel. To hinder this work should be the sole policy of all those who are interested in their personal existence, in the principality, in the Princess, and possibly even in the Prince.

CHAMBERLAIN: "Possibly even"— you're very candid. To be equally frank, your candor makes me tremble at the imminent decision. And I regret, as I've recently come to regret more and more,

172

that I'm devoted to the Prince almost to the point of helplessness.

S T E W A R D : Everything is clear. You are not flirting with the opposition. In fact, you are even holding out a hand. Only one, which is commendable for an old courtier. And yet your only hope is that our great example carries you along.

C H A M B E R L A I N : Whatever I can do to prevent it, I shall do.

S T E W A R D : It doesn't frighten me any more. (*Pointing to the Warden.*) And you who've been sitting there so quietly, have you understood everything that's been said?

C H A M B E R L A I N : The Warden of the tomb?

S T E W A R D : The Warden of the tomb. One must probably be a stranger to size him up. Isn't that so, old boy, you little old screech-owl, you! Have you ever seen him flying through the forest in the evening, out of any gun's reach? But by day he ducks at the slightest move.

C H A M B E R L A I N : I don't understand.

W A R D E N (*almost in tears*): You're scolding me, sir, and I don't know why. Please let me go home. I'm really not evil, I'm just the Warden of the tomb.

C H A M B E R L A I N : You mistrust him.

S T E W A R D : Mistrust? No, he's too insignificant for that. But I want to keep an eye on him. For I think—call it whim or superstition, if you like—that he's not just a mere tool of evil, but an upright, active worker for evil.

C H A M B E R L A I N : He has been serving the Court quietly for thirty years—possibly without ever having been in the castle.

S T E W A R D : Oh, moles like him build long passages before they emerge. (*Suddenly turns to Warden.*) But first of all, away with this one! (*To servant*) Take him to the Friedrichspark, stay with him, and don't let him out until further notice.

W A R D E N (*very frightened*): I'm supposed to wait for his Highness, the Prince.

S T E W A R D : An error.—Off with you.

CHAMBERLAIN: He must be treated with care. He's an old and sick man, and for some reason the Prince sets store by him.

WARDEN (*bowing low before Chamberlain*).

STEWARD: What? (*To servant*) Treat him carefully, but for God's sake get him out of here. Quick!

SERVANT (*about to grab him*).

CHAMBERLAIN (*stepping between them*): No, we must get a carriage.

STEWARD: It's the air at this Court. I can't taste a grain of salt anywhere. All right then, a carriage. You take the treasure away in a carriage. But now, out of the room with you both! (*To Chamberlain*) Your behavior shows me——

WARDEN (*collapses, with a little scream, on way to door*).

STEWARD (*stamping his foot*): Is it impossible to get rid of him? Pick him up in your arms if there's no other way. Can't you understand what's expected of you!

C H A M B E R L A I N : The Prince!

S E R V A N T (*opening door at left*).

S T E W A R D : Ah! (*Glances at Warden.*) I should have known that ghosts cannot be transported.

P R I N C E (*enters with quick steps, behind him the Princess, dark young woman with teeth clenched, stops in doorway*).

P R I N C E : What's happened?

S T E W A R D : The Warden felt ill, I was about to have him taken away.

P R I N C E : I should have been notified. Has the doctor been sent for?

C H A M B E R L A I N : I'll have him called. (*Hurries out by center door, returns at once.*)

P R I N C E (*kneeling beside Warden*): Prepare a bed for him! Fetch a stretcher! Is the doctor on his way? He's taking a long time. The pulse is very weak. I can't hear the heart. These miserable ribs! How worn out this body is! (*Stands up suddenly, fetches a glass of water, stares about him.*) One is so helpless. (*Kneels down again, moistens the Warden's face.*) Now he's breathing better. It won't be so bad. Healthy stock, the kind that doesn't give up, even in extremity. But the doctor, the doctor! (*While he glances towards the door, the Warden raises his hand and caresses the Prince's cheek. Princess turns her head away, towards the window. Enter servants with stretcher, Prince helps to lift Warden.*)

P R I N C E : Handle him gently. Oh, you with your great claws! Lift his head a little. Nearer the stretcher. The pillow further down his back. His arm! His arm! You're all bad, bad nurses! I wonder if you'll ever be as tired as this man on the stretcher?—There we are—and now with slow—slow—steps. And above all, steadily. (*Turning in door to Princess*) Here then is the Warden of the tomb.

P R I N C E S S (*nods*).

P R I N C E : I had intended to show him to you differently. (*After taking another step*) Aren't you coming along?

P R I N C E S S : I'm so tired.

177

PRINCE : The moment I've talked to the doctor I'll come back. And you, gentlemen, who wish to make your report, wait for me.

STEWARD (*to Princess*): Does your Highness require my services?

PRINCESS : Always. I am grateful for your vigilance. Do not abandon it, even if today it was in vain. Everything is at stake. You see more than I. I am always in my rooms. But I know it will get more and more gloomy. This autumn is sad beyond belief.

THE REFUSAL

Our little town does not lie on the frontier, no-
where near; it is so far from the frontier, in
fact, that perhaps no one from our town has
ever been there; desolate highlands have to
be crossed as well as wide fertile plains. To
imagine even part of the road makes one tired,
and more than part one just cannot imagine.
There are also big towns on the road, each
far larger than ours. Ten little towns like ours
laid side by side, and ten more forced down
from above, still would not produce one of
these enormous, overcrowded towns. If one
does not get lost on the way one is bound to
lose oneself in these towns, and to avoid them
is impossible on account of their size.

But what is even further from our town than
the frontier, if such distances can be compared at all—it's like saying that a man of
three hundred years is older than one of two
hundred—what is even further than the frontier is the capital. Whereas we do get news

of the frontier wars now and again, of the capital we learn next to nothing—we civilians that is, for of course the government officials have very good connections with the capital; they can get news from there in as little as three months, so they claim at least.

Now it is remarkable and I am continually being surprised by the way we in our town humbly submit to all orders issued in the capital. For centuries no political change has been brought about by the citizens themselves. In the capital great rulers have superseded each other—indeed, even dynasties have been deposed or annihilated, and new ones have started; in the past century even the capital itself was destroyed, a new one was founded far away from it, later on this too was destroyed and the old one rebuilt, yet none of this had any influence on our little town. Our officials have always remained at their posts; the highest officials came from the capital, the less high from other towns, and the lowest from among ourselves that is how it has always been and it has suited us. The highest official is the chief tax-collector, he has the rank of colonel, and is known as such. The present one is an old man; I've known him for years, because he was already a colonel when I was a child. At first he rose very fast in his career, but then he seems to have advanced no further; actually, for our little town his rank is good enough, a higher rank would be out of place. When I try to recall him I see him sitting on the veranda of his house in the Market Square, leaning back, pipe in mouth. Above him from the roof flutters the imperial flag; on the sides of the veranda, which is so big that minor military maneuvers are sometimes held there, washing hangs out to dry. His grandchildren, in beautiful silk clothes, play around him; they are not allowed down in the Market Square, the children there are considered unworthy of them, but the grandchildren are attracted by the Square, so they thrust their heads between the posts of the banister and when the children below begin to quarrel they join the quarrel from above.

This colonel, then, commands the town. I don't think he has ever produced a document entitling him to this position; very likely he does not possess such a thing. Maybe he really is chief tax-collector. But is that all? Does that entitle him to rule over all the other departments in the administration as well? True, his office is very important for the government, but for the citizens it is hardly the most important. One is almost under the impression that the people here say: "Now that you've taken all we possess, please take us as well." In reality, of course, it was not he who seized the power, nor is he a tyrant. It has just come about over the years that the chief tax-collector is automatically the top official, and the colonel accepts the tradition just as we do.

Yet while he lives among us without laying too much stress on his official position, he is something quite different from the ordinary citizen. When a delegation comes to him with a request, he stands there like the wall of the world. Behind him is nothingness, one imagines hearing voices whispering in the background, but this is probably a delusion; after all, he represents the end of all things, at least for us. At these receptions he really was worth seeing. Once as a child I was present when a

184

delegation of citizens arrived to ask him for a government subsidy because the poorest quarter of the town had been burned to the ground. My father the blacksmith, a man well respected in the community, was a member of the delegation and had taken me along. There's nothing exceptional about this, everyone rushes to spectacles of this kind, one can hardly distinguish the actual delegation from the crowd. Since these receptions usually take place on the veranda, there are even people who climb up by ladder from the Market Square and take part in the goings-on from over the banister. On this occasion about a quarter of the veranda had been reserved for the colonel, the crowd filling the rest of it. A few soldiers kept watch, some of them standing round him in a semicircle. Actually a single soldier would have been quite enough, such is our fear of them. I don't know exactly where these soldiers come from, in any case from a long way off, they all look very much alike, they wouldn't even need a uniform. They are small, not strong but agile people, the most striking thing about them is the

prominence of their teeth which almost over-
crowd their mouths, and a certain restless
twitching of their small narrow eyes. This
makes them the terror of the children, but also
their delight, for again and again the children
long to be frightened by these teeth, these eyes,
so as to be able to run away in horror. Even
grownups probably never quite lose this child-
ish terror, at least it continues to have an effect. There are, of course, other factors contrib-
uting to it. The soldiers speak a dialect
utterly incomprehensible to us, and they can
hardly get used to ours—all of which produces
a certain shut-off, unapproachable quality
corresponding, as it happens, to their character, for they are silent, serious, and rigid. They
don't actually do anything evil, and yet they
are almost unbearable in an evil sense. A soldier, for example, enters a shop, buys some
trifling object, and stays there leaning against
the counter; he listens to the conversations,
probably does not understand them, and yet
gives the impression of understanding; he
himself does not say a word, just stares
blankly at the speaker, then back at the lis-

teners, all the while keeping his hand on the hilt of the long knife in his belt. This is revolting, one loses the desire to talk, the customers start leaving the shop, and only when it is quite empty does the soldier also leave. Thus wherever the soldiers appear, our lively people grow silent. That's what happened this time, too. As on all solemn occasions the colonel stood upright, holding in front of him two poles of bamboo in his outstretched hands. This is an ancient custom implying more or less that he supports the law, and the law supports him. Now everyone knows, of course, what to expect up on the veranda, and yet each time people take fright all over again. On this occasion, too, the man chosen to speak could not begin; he was already standing opposite the colonel when his courage failed him and, muttering a few excuses, he pushed his way back into the crowd. No other suitable person willing to speak could be found, albeit several unsuitable ones offered themselves; a great commotion ensued and messengers were sent in search of various citizens who were well-known speakers. During all this time the colonel stood there motionless, only his chest moving visibly up and down to his breathing. Not that he breathed with difficulty, it was just that he breathed so conspicuously, much as frogs breathe—except that with them it is normal, while here it was exceptional. I squeezed myself through the grownups and watched him through a gap between two soldiers, until one of them kicked me away with his knee. Meanwhile the man originally chosen to speak had regained his composure and, firmly held up by two fellow citizens, was delivering his address. It was touching to see him smile throughout this solemn speech describing a grievous misfortune—a most humble smile which strove in vain to elicit some slight reaction on the colonel's face. Finally he formulated the request—I think he was only asking for a year's tax exemption, but possibly also for timber from the imperial forests at a reduced price. Then he bowed low, remaining in this position for some time, as did everyone else except the colonel, the soldiers, and a number of officials in the background. To the child it seemed ridiculous that the people on

the ladders should climb down a few rungs
so as not to be seen during the significant
pause and now and again peer inquisitively
over the floor of the veranda. After this had
lasted quite a while an official, a little man,
stepped up to the colonel and tried to reach
the latter's height by standing on his toes. The
colonel, still motionless save for his deep
breathing, whispered something in his ear,
whereupon the little man clapped his hands
and everyone rose. "The petition has been refused," he announced. "You may go." An un-
deniable sense of relief passed through the
crowd, everyone surged out, hardly a soul paying any special attention to the colonel, who,
as it were, had turned once more into a human
being like the rest of us. I still caught one
last glimpse of him as he wearily let go of
the poles, which fell to the ground, then sank
into an armchair produced by some officials,
and promptly put his pipe in his mouth.

This whole occurrence is not isolated, it's in
the general run of things. Indeed, it does happen now and again that minor petitions are
granted, but then it invariably looks as though

the colonel had done it as a powerful private person on his own responsibility, and it had to be kept all but a secret from the government —not explicitly of course, but that is what it feels like. No doubt in our little town the colonel's eyes, so far as we know, are also the eyes of the government, and yet there is a difference which it is impossible to comprehend completely.

In all important matters, however, the citizens can always count on a refusal. And now the strange fact is that without this refusal one simply cannot get along, yet at the same time these official occasions designed to receive the refusal are by no means a formality. Time after time one goes there full of expectation and in all seriousness and then one returns, if not exactly strengthened or happy, nevertheless not disappointed or tired. About these things I do not have to ask the opinion of anyone else, I feel them in myself, as everyone does; nor do I have any great desire to find out how these things are connected.

As a matter of fact there is, so far as my observations go, a certain age group that is not content—these are the young people roughly between seventeen and twenty. Quite young fellows, in fact, who are utterly incapable of foreseeing the consequences of even the least significant, far less a revolutionary, idea. And it is among just them that discontent creeps in.

SHORT PIECES

Poseidon

Poseidon sat at his desk, going over the accounts. The administration of all the waters gave him endless work. He could have had as many assistants as he wanted, and indeed he had quite a number, but since he took his job very seriously he insisted on going through all the accounts again himself, and so his assistants were of little help to him. It cannot be said that he enjoyed the work; he carried it out simply because it was assigned to him; indeed he had frequently applied for what he called more cheerful work, but whenever various suggestions were put to him it turned out that nothing suited him so well as his present employment. Needless to say, it was very difficult to find him another job. After all, he could not possibly be put in charge of one particular ocean. Quite apart from the fact that in this case the work involved would not be less, only more petty, the great Poseidon could hold only a superior position. And when he was offered a post unrelated to the waters, the very idea made him feel sick, his divine breath came short and his brazen chest began to heave. As a matter of fact, no one took his troubles very seriously; when a mighty man complains one must pretend to yield, however hopeless the case may seem. No one ever really considered relieving Poseidon of his position; he had been destined to be God of the Seas since time immemorial, and that was how it had to remain.

What annoyed him most—and this was the chief cause of discontent with his job—was to learn of the rumors that were circulating about him; for instance, that he was constantly cruising through the waves with his trident. Instead of which here he was sitting in the depths of the world's ocean endlessly going over the accounts, an occasional journey to Jupiter being the only interruption of the monotony, a journey moreover from which he invariably returned in a furious temper. As a result he had hardly seen the oceans, save fleetingly during his hasty ascent to Olympus, and had never really sailed upon them. He used to say that he was postponing this until

196

the end of the world, for then there might come a quiet moment when, just before the end and having gone through the last account, he could still make a quick little tour.

The Vulture

A vulture was hacking at my feet. It had already torn my boots and stockings to shreds, now it was hacking at the feet themselves. Again and again it struck at them, then circled several times restlessly round me, then returned to continue its work. A gentleman passed by, looked on for a while, then asked me why I suffered the vulture. "I'm helpless," I said. "When it came and began to attack me, I of course tried to drive it away, even to strangle it, but these animals are very strong, it was about to spring at my face, but I preferred to sacrifice my feet. Now they are almost torn to bits." "Fancy letting yourself be tortured like this!" said the gentleman. "One shot and that's the end of the vulture." "Really?" I said. "And would you do that?" "With pleasure," said the gentleman, "I've only got to go home and get my gun. Could you wait another half hour?" "I'm not sure about that," said I, and stood for a moment rigid with pain. Then I said: "Do try it in any case, please." "Very well," said the gentleman, "I'll be as quick as I can." During this conversation the vulture had been calmly listening, letting its eye rove between me and the gentleman. Now I realized that it had understood everything; it took wing, leaned far back to gain impetus, and then, like a javelin thrower, thrust its beak through my mouth, deep into me. Falling back, I was relieved to feel him drowning irretrievably in my blood, which was filling every depth, flooding every shore.

The Departure

I ordered my horse to be brought from the
stables. The servant did not understand my
orders. So I went to the stables myself, saddled
my horse, and mounted. In the distance I heard
the sound of a trumpet, and I asked the servant
what it meant. He knew nothing and had heard
nothing. At the gate he stopped me and asked:
"Where is the master going?" "I don't know,"
I said, "just out of here, just out of here. Out
of here, nothing else, it's the only way I can
reach my goal." "So you know your goal?" he
asked. "Yes," I replied, "I've just told you.
Out of here—that's my goal."

Give It Up!

It was very early in the morning, the streets clean and deserted, I was on my way to the station. As I compared the tower clock with my watch I realized it was much later than I had thought and that I had to hurry; the shock of this discovery made me feel uncertain of the way, I wasn't very well acquainted with the town as yet; fortunately, there was a policeman at hand, I ran to him and breathlessly asked him the way. He smiled and said: "You asking me the way?" "Yes," I said, "since I can't find it myself." "Give it up! Give it up!" said he, and turned with a sudden jerk, like someone who wants to be alone with his laughter.

At Night

Deeply lost in the night. Just as one sometimes lowers one's head to reflect, thus to be utterly lost in the night. All around people are asleep. It's just play acting, an innocent self-deception, that they sleep in houses, in safe beds, under a safe roof, stretched out or curled up on mattresses, in sheets, under blankets; in reality they have flocked together as they had once upon a time and again later in a deserted region, a camp in the open, a countless number of men, an army, a people, under a cold sky on cold earth, collapsed where once they had stood, forehead pressed on the arm, face to the ground, breathing quietly. And you are watching, are one of the watchmen, you find the next one by brandishing a burning stick from the brushwood pile beside you. Why are you watching? Someone must watch, it is said. Someone must be there.

The Helmsman

"Am I not the helmsman here?" I called out.
"You?" asked a tall dark man and passed his
hands over his eyes as though to banish a
dream. I had been standing at the helm in the
dark night, a feeble lantern burning over my
head, and now this man had come and tried to
push me aside. And as I would not yield, he put
his foot on my chest and slowly crushed me
while I still clung to the hub of the helm,
wrenching it round in falling. But the man
seized it, pulled it back in place, and pushed
me away. I soon collected myself, however, ran
to the hatchway which gave on to the mess
quarters, and cried out: "Men! Comrades!
Come here, quick! A stranger has driven me
away from the helm!" Slowly they came up,
climbing the companion ladder, tired, swaying,
powerful figures. "Am I the helmsman?" I
asked. They nodded, but they had eyes only
for the stranger, stood round him in a semicircle, and when, in a commanding voice, he
said: "Don't disturb me!" they gathered to-

gether, nodded at me, and withdrew down the companion ladder. What kind of people are these? Do they ever think, or do they only shuffle pointlessly over the earth?

The Top

A certain philosopher used to hang about wherever children were at play. And whenever he saw a boy with a top, he would lie in wait. As soon as the top began to spin the philosopher went in pursuit and tried to catch it. He was not perturbed when the children noisily protested and tried to keep him away from their toy; so long as he could catch the top while it was still spinning, he was happy, but only for a moment; then he threw it to the ground and walked away. For he believed that the understanding of any detail, that of a spinning top, for instance, was sufficient for the understanding of all things. For this reason he did not busy himself with great problems, it seemed to him uneconomical. Once the smallest detail was understood, then everything was understood, which was why he busied himself only with the spinning top. And whenever preparations were being made for the spinning of the top, he hoped that this time it would succeed: as soon as the top began to spin and he was running breathlessly after it, the hope would turn to certainty, but when he held the silly piece of wood in his hand, he felt nauseated. The screaming of the children, which hitherto he had not heard and which now suddenly pierced his ears, chased him away, and he tottered like a top under a clumsy whip.

The Test

I am a servant, but there is no work for me. I am timid and don't push myself to the fore, indeed I don't even push myself into line with the others, but that is only one reason for my nonemployment, it's even possible that it has nothing to do with my nonemployment, in any case the main thing is that I am not called upon to serve, others have been called yet they have not tried harder than I, indeed perhaps they have not even felt the desire to be called, whereas I, at least sometimes, have felt it very strongly.

So I lie on the pallet in the servants' hall, stare at the beams in the ceiling, fall asleep, wake up and promptly fall asleep again. Occasionally I walk over to the tavern where they sell a sour beer, occasionally I have even poured away a glass in disgust, but at other times I drink it. I like sitting there because from behind the closed little window, without the possibility of being discovered, I can see across to the windows of our house. Not that one sees very much there, to my knowledge only the windows of the corridors look out on the street, and moreover not even those of the corridors leading to my employers' apartments. But it is also possible that I am mistaken; someone, without my having asked him, once said so, and the general impression of this house front confirms this. Only rarely are the windows opened, and when this does occur it is done by a servant who may lean against the balustrade to look down for a while. It follows therefore that these are corridors where he cannot be taken by surprise. As a matter of fact I am not personally acquainted with these servants; those who are permanently employed upstairs sleep elsewhere, not in my room.

Once when I arrived at the tavern, a guest was sitting at my observation post. I did not dare look at him closely and was about to turn round in the door and leave. The guest, however, called me over, and it turned out that he too was a servant whom I had once seen somewhere before, but without having spoken to him.

"Why do you want to run away? Sit down

and have a drink! I'll pay." So I sat down. He asked me several things, but I couldn't answer, indeed I didn't even understand his questions. So I said: "Perhaps you are sorry now that you invited me, so I'd better go," and I was about to get up. But he stretched his hand out over the table and pressed me down. "Stay," he said, "that was only a test. He who does not answer the questions has passed the test."

Advocates

I was not at all certain whether I had any advocates, I could not find out anything definite about it, every face was unfriendly, most people who came towards me and whom I kept meeting in the corridors looked like fat old women; they had huge blue and white striped aprons covering their entire bodies, kept stroking their stomachs and swaying awkwardly to and fro. I could not even find out whether we were in a law court. Some facts spoke for it, others against. What reminded me of a law court more than all the details was a droning noise which could be heard incessantly in the distance; one could not tell from which direction it came, it filled every room to such an extent that one had to assume it came from everywhere or, what seemed more likely, that just the place where one happened to be standing was the very place where the droning originated, but this was probably an illusion, for it came from a distance. These corridors, narrow and austerely vaulted, turning

in gradual curves with high, sparsely decorated doors, seemed to have been created spe-
cially for profound silence; they were the corridors of a museum or a library. Yet if it were
not a law court, why was I searching for an
advocate here? Because I was searching for
an advocate everywhere; he is needed everywhere, if anything less in court than elsewhere,
for a court, one assumes, passes judgment according to the law. If one were to assume that
this was being done unfairly or frivolously,
then life would not be possible; one must have
confidence that the court allows the majesty
of the law its full scope, for this is its sole duty.
Within the law all is accusation, advocacy, and
verdict; any interference by an individual here
would be a crime. It is different, however, in
the case of the verdict itself; this is based on
inquiries being made here and there, from relatives and strangers, from friends and ene-
mies, in the family and public life, in town
and village—in short, everywhere. Here it is
most necessary to have advocates, advocates
galore, the best possible advocates, one next
to the other, a living wall, for advocates are

by nature hard to set in motion; the plaintiffs, however, those sly foxes, those slinking weasels, those little mice, they slip through the tiniest gaps, scuttle through the legs of the advocates. So look out! That's why I am here, I'm collecting advocates. But I have not found any as yet, only those old women keep on coming and going; if I were not on my search it would put me to sleep. I'm not in the right place—alas, I cannot rid myself of the feeling that I'm not in the right place. I ought to be in a place where all kinds of people meet, from various parts of the country, from every class, every profession, of all ages; I ought to have an opportunity of choosing carefully out of a crowd those who are kind, those who are able, and those who have an eye for me. Perhaps the most suitable place for this would be a huge fair-ground; instead of which I am hanging about in these corridors where only these old women are to be seen, and not even many of them, and always the same ones, and even those few will not let themselves be cornered, despite their slowness; they slip away from me, float about like rain clouds, and are

completely absorbed by unknown activities.
Why is it then that I run headlong into a house
without reading the sign over the door,
promptly find myself in these corridors, and
settle here with such obstinacy that I cannot
even remember ever having been in front of
the house, ever having run up the stairs! But
back I cannot go, this waste of time, this ad-
mission of having been on the wrong track
would be unbearable for me. What? Run downstairs in this brief, hurried life accompanied as
it is by that impatient droning? Impossible.
The time allotted to you is so short that if you
lose one second you have already lost your
whole life, for it is no longer, it is always just
as long as the time you lose. So if you have
started out on a walk, continue it whatever
happens; you can only gain, you run no risk,
in the end you may fall over a precipice perhaps, but had you turned back after the first
steps and run downstairs you would have fallen at once—and not perhaps, but for certain.
So if you find nothing in the corridors open
the doors, if you find nothing behind these
doors there are more floors, and if you find

nothing up there, don't worry, just leap up another flight of stairs. As long as you don't stop climbing the stairs won't end, under your climbing feet they will go on growing upwards.

Home-Coming

I have returned, I have passed under the arch and am looking around. It's my father's old yard. The puddle in the middle. Old, useless tools, jumbled together, block the way to the attic stairs. The cat lurks on the banister. A torn piece of cloth, once wound round a stick in a game, flutters in the breeze. I have arrived. Who is going to receive me? Who is waiting behind the kitchen door? Smoke is rising from the chimney, coffee is being made for supper. Do you feel you belong, do you feel at home? I don't know, I feel most uncertain. My father's house it is, but each object stands cold beside the next, as though preoccupied with its own affairs, which I have partly forgotten, partly never known. What use can I be to them, what do I mean to them, even though I am the son of my father, the old farmer? And I don't dare knock at the kitchen door, I only listen from a distance, I only listen from a distance, standing up, in such a way that I cannot be taken by surprise as an eavesdropper. And since I am listening from a distance, I hear nothing but a faint striking of the clock passing over from childhood days, but perhaps I only think I hear it. Whatever else is going on in the kitchen is the secret of those sitting there, a secret they are keeping from me. The longer one hesitates before the door, the more estranged one becomes. What would happen if someone were to open the door now and ask me a question? Would not I myself then behave like one who wants to keep his secret?

Fellowship

We are five friends, one day we came out of a house one after the other, first one came and placed himself beside the gate, then the second came, or rather he glided through the gate like a little ball of quicksilver, and placed himself near the first one, then came the third, then the fourth, then the fifth. Finally we all stood in a row. People began to notice us, they pointed at us and said: Those five just came out of that house. Since then we have been living together; it would be a peaceful life if it weren't for a sixth one continually trying to interfere. He doesn't do us any harm, but he annoys us, and that is harm enough; why does he intrude where he is not wanted? We don't know him and don't want him to join us. There was a time, of course, when the five of us did not know one another, either; and it could be said that we still don't know one another, but what is possible and can be tolerated by the five of us is not possible and cannot be tolerated with this sixth one. In any case, we are five and don't want to be six. And what is the point of this continual being together anyhow? It is also pointless for the five of us, but here we are together and will remain together; a new combination, however, we do not want, just because of our experiences. But how is one to make all this clear to the sixth one? Long explanations would almost amount to accepting him in our circle, so we prefer not to explain and not to accept him. No matter how he pouts his lips we push him away with our elbows, but however much we push him away, back he comes.

FRAGMENTS OF

A Report to an Academy

We all know Rotpeter, just as half the world
knows him. But when he came to our town for
a guest performance, I decided to get to know
him personally. It is not difficult to be admitted. In big cities where everyone in the
know clamors to watch celebrities breathe
from as close as possible, great difficulties may
be encountered; but in our town one is content
to marvel at the marvellous from the pit. Thus
I was the only one so far, as the hotel servant
told me, to have announced his visit. Herr
Busenau, the impresario, received me with extreme courtesy. I had not expected to meet a
man so modest, indeed almost timid. He was
sitting in the anteroom of Rotpeter's apartment, eating an omelet. Although it was
morning he already sat there in the evening
clothes in which he appears at the perform-
ances. Hardly had he caught sight of me—me
the unknown, the unimportant guest—when

he, possessor of highly distinguished medals, king of trainers, honorary doctor of great universities, jumped up, shook me by both hands, urged me to sit down, wiped his spoon on the tablecloth, and amiably offered it to me so that I might finish his omelet. He would not accept my grateful refusal and promptly tried to feed me. I had some trouble calming him down and warding him off, as well as his spoon and plate.

"Very kind of you to have come," he said with a strong foreign accent. "Most kind. You've also come at the right time, for alas Rotpeter cannot always receive. Seeing people is often repugnant to him; on these occasions no one, it does not matter who he may be, is admitted; then I, even I can see him only on business, so to speak, on the stage. And immediately after the performance I have to disappear, he drives home alone, locks himself in his room, and usually remains like that until the following evening. He always has a big hamper of fruit in his bedroom, this is what he lives on at these times. But I, who of course dare not let him out of my sight, always rent

the apartment opposite his and watch him
from behind curtains."

When I sit opposite you like this, Rotpeter,
listening to you talk, drinking your health, I
really and truly forget—whether you take it as
a compliment or not, it's the truth—that you
are a chimpanzee. Only gradually, when I
have forced myself out of my thoughts back to
reality, do my eyes show me again whose
guest I am.

Yes.

You're so silent suddenly, I wonder why?
Just a moment ago you were pronouncing such
astonishingly correct opinions about our town,
and now you're so silent.

Silent?

Is something wrong? Shall I call the
trainer? Perhaps you're in the habit of taking
a meal at this hour?

No, no. It's quite all right. I can tell you
what it was. Sometimes I'm overcome with
such an aversion to human beings that I can
barely refrain from retching. This, of course,

221

has nothing to do with the individual human being, least of all with your charming presence. It concerns all human beings. There's nothing extraordinary about this. Suppose, for instance, that you were to live continuously with apes, you'd probably have similar attacks, however great your self-control. Actually, it's not the smell of human beings which repels me so much, it's the human smell which I have contracted and which mingles with the smell from my native land. Smell for yourself! Here, on my chest! Put your nose deeper into the fur! Deeper, I say!

I'm sorry, but I can't smell anything special. Just the ordinary smell of a well-groomed body, that's all. The nose of a city-dweller, of course, is no fair test. You, no doubt, can scent thousands of things that evade us.

Once upon a time, sir, once upon a time. That's over.

Since you brought it up yourself, I dare to ask: How long have you actually been living among us?

Five years. On the fifth of April it will be five years.

Terrific achievement. To cast off apehood in five years and gallop through the whole evolution of mankind! Certainly no one has ever done that before! On this racecourse you have no rival.

It's a great deal, I know, and sometimes it surpasses even my understanding. In tranquil moments, however, I feel less exuberant about it. Do you know how I was caught?

I've read everything that's been printed about you. You were shot at and then caught.

Yes, I was hit twice, once here in the cheek —the wound of course was far larger than the scar you see—and the second time below the hip. I'll take my trousers down so you can see that scar, too. Here then was where the bullet entered; this was the severe, decisive wound. I fell from the tree and when I came to I was in a cage between decks.

In a cage! Between decks! It's one thing to read your story, and quite another to hear you tell it!

And yet another, sir, to have experienced it. Until then I had never known what it means to have no way out. It was not a four-sided barred cage, it had only three sides nailed to a locker, the locker forming the fourth side. The whole contrivance was so low that I could not stand upright, and so narrow that I could not even sit down. All I could do was squat there with bent knees. In my rage I refused to see anyone, and so remained facing the locker; for days and nights I squatted there with trembling knees while behind me the bars cut into my flesh. This manner of confining wild animals is considered to have its advantages during the first days of captivity, and from my experience I cannot deny that from the human point of view this actually is the case. But at that time I was not interested in the human point of view. I had the locker in front of me. Break the boards, bite a hole through them, squeeze yourself through an opening which in reality hardly allows you to see through it and which, when you first discover it, you greet with the blissful howl of ignorance! Where do you want to go? Beyond the boards the forest begins. . . .

(*Beginning of a Letter*)

Dear Herr Rotpeter:

I have read the report which you wrote for the Academy of Science with great interest, indeed with a beating heart. Small wonder, since I was your first teacher, and since you have found such kind words with which to express your memory of me. With some consideration it might perhaps have been possible to avoid mentioning my sojourn in the sanitarium; I realize, however, that your whole report and the frankness which characterizes it could not omit this small detail once it had occurred to you while writing, although it does compromise me somewhat. However, this isn't really what I wanted to talk about here, I have other things on my mind.

FRAGMENT OF

The Great Wall of China

The news of the building of the wall now penetrated into this world—late, too, some thirty
years after its announcement. It was on a summer evening. I, ten years old, was standing
with my father on the riverbank. In keeping
with the importance of this much-discussed
hour, I can recall the smallest details. My father was holding me by the hand, something
he was fond of doing to the end of his days,
and running his other hand up and down his
long, very thin pipe, as though it were a flute.
With his sparse, rigid beard raised in the air,
he was enjoying his pipe while gazing upwards across the river. As a result his pigtail,
object of the children's veneration, sank lower,
rustling faintly on the gold-embroidered silk
of his holiday gown. At that moment a barque
drew up before us, the boatman beckoned to
my father to come down the embankment,
while he himself climbed up towards him.

226

They met halfway, the boatman whispered
something in my father's ear, in order to come
quite close he had embraced him. I could not
understand what they said, I only saw that
my father did not seem to believe the news,
that the boatman tried to insist upon its truth,
that when my father still refused to believe it
the boatman, with the passion of sailors, almost tore the garment from his chest to prove
the truth, whereupon my father fell silent and
the boatman jumped noisily into the barque
and sailed away. Deep in thought my father
turned toward me, knocked his pipe out and
stuck it in his belt, stroked my cheek, and
pulled my head toward him. That is what I
liked best, it made me very happy, and so we
came home. There the rice-pap was already
steaming on the table, several guests had assembled, the wine was just being poured into
the goblets. Paying no attention to any of this
and having advanced no further than the
threshold, my father started telling what he
had heard. Of the exact words I have of course
no recollection, but owing to the exceptional
circumstances which cast a spell even over the

child, the meaning became so clear to me that I venture nevertheless to give some version of what my father said. I am doing so because it was very characteristic of the popular point of view. My father said something like this: An unknown boatman—I know all those who usually pass by here, but this one was a stranger —has just told me that a great wall is going to be built to protect the Emperor. For it seems that infidel tribes, among them demons, often assemble before the imperial palace and shoot their black arrows at the Emperor.

The Conscription of Troops

The conscription of troops, often necessary on account of the never-ending frontier wars, takes place in the following manner:

The order goes out that on a certain day in a certain part of town all inhabitants—men, women, and children without exception—have to remain indoors. Usually at about noon the young nobleman in charge of the conscription appears at the entrance of that part of town where a detachment of soldiers, both infantry and cavalry, has been waiting since dawn. He is a young man, slender, not tall, weak, carelessly dressed, with tired eyes, waves of restlessness continually passing through him like the shivers of a fever. Without looking at anyone he makes a sign with a whip, his sole equipment, whereupon several soldiers join him and he enters the first house. A soldier, who knows personally all the inhabitants in this part of town, reads out the list of the inmates. As a rule they are all present, lined up in the room, their eyes fixed on the nobleman, as though they were soldiers already. It can happen, however, that here and there someone, it's invariably a man, is missing. In this case no one will dare to utter an excuse, let alone a lie, everyone is silent, all eyes are lowered, the pressure of the command which someone in this house has evaded is almost unbearable, but the silent presence of the nobleman keeps everyone nevertheless in his place. The nobleman makes a sign, it's not even a nod, it can be read only in his eyes, and two soldiers begin the search for the missing man. This is not difficult. He is never out of the house, never really intends to evade military service, it's only fear that has prevented him from turning up, yet it's not fear of the service itself that keeps him away, it's the general reluctance to show himself, for him the command is almost too great, so frighteningly great that he cannot appear of his own accord. This is why he does not flee, he simply goes into hiding, and on learning that the nobleman is in the house he even leaves his hiding place and creeps to the door of the room where he is promptly caught by the soldiers in search of him. He is brought before the nobleman who seizes the whip with both hands—he is so weak he can't do it with one hand—and gives the man a thrashing. Having inflicted no great pain, he drops the whip, half from exhaustion, half from disgust, whereupon the beaten man has to pick it up and hand it to him. Only then may he join the line with the others; incidentally, it is almost certain that he will not be recruited. But it also happens, and this is more frequent, that a greater number of people appear than are listed. There, for instance, stands an unknown girl, staring at the nobleman; she is from out of town, from the provinces perhaps, the conscription has lured her here. There are many women who cannot resist the temptation of a conscription in another town, conscriptions at home meaning something quite different. And, strangely enough, it is not considered disgraceful for a woman to surrender to this temptation; on the contrary, in the opinion of many, this is something women have to go through, a debt which they pay to their sex. Moreover, it invariably takes the same course. The girl or the woman learns that somewhere, perhaps very far away, at the home of relatives or friends, a conscription is going to take place; she asks her family for permission to undertake the journey, which is granted—it cannot very well be refused—she puts on her best clothes, is gayer than usual, at the same time calm and friendly, no matter what she may be like at other times; and yet behind all the calm and friendliness she is inaccessible, like an utter stranger who is on her way home and can think of nothing else. In the family where the conscription is going to take place she is received quite differently from an ordinary guest; everyone flatters her, she is invited to walk through all the rooms in the house, lean out of all the windows, and if she puts her hand on someone's head it means more than a father's blessing. When the family is preparing for the conscription she is given the best place, which is near the door where she has the best chance of being seen by the nobleman and can best see him. She is honored in this way, however, only until the nobleman enters; thereafter she begins to fade. He looks at her as little as at the

others, and even when his eye rests on someone, that person is not aware of being looked
at. This is something she has not expected or
rather she certainly has, for it cannot be otherwise, yet it wasn't the expectation of the opposite that had driven her here, it was just
something that had now definitely come to an
end. She feels shame to a degree which our
women possibly feel at no other time; only now
is she fully aware of having forced her way into
a foreign conscription, and when the soldier
has read out the list and her name is not on it
and there comes a moment of silence, she flees
stooped and trembling out of the door, receiv-
ing in addition a blow in the back from a soldier's fist.

Should the person not on the list be a man,
his only desire is to be conscripted with the
others although he does not belong to this
house. But this too is utterly out of the question, an outsider of this kind has never been
conscripted and nothing of the sort will ever
happen.

FRAGMENT OF
The Hunter Gracchus

Is it true, Hunter Gracchus, that you have been
cruising about in this old boat for hundreds of
years?

For fifteen hundred years.

And always in this ship?

Always in this bark. Bark, I believe, is the
correct expression. You aren't familiar with
nautical matters?

No, I never gave them a thought until today,
until I heard about you, until I boarded your
ship.

Don't apologize. I'm from the interior, too.
Never been a seafarer, never wanted to be one,
mountains and forests were my friends, and
now—most ancient of seafarers, Hunter Gracchus, patron saint of sailors, Hunter Gracchus
—the cabin boy shivering with fear in the
crow's-nest in the stormy night prays to me
with wringing hands. Don't laugh.

Me laugh? Certainly not. With a beating

heart I stood before your cabin door, with a beating heart I entered. Your friendly manner has calmed me a little, but I'll never forget whose guest I am.

You're right, of course. However it may be, I am Hunter Gracchus. Won't you drink some wine? I don't know the brand, but it's sweet and heavy, the master does me proud.

Not just now, I'm too restless. Later perhaps, if you can bear with me that long. Besides, I wouldn't dare drink out of your glass. Who is the master?

The owner of the bark. They are excellent men, these masters. Except that I don't understand them. I don't mean their language, although of course I often don't understand their language, either. But this is beside the point. Over the centuries I've learned enough languages to act as interpreter between this generation and their ancestors. What I don't understand is the way the masters' minds work. Perhaps you can explain it to me.

I haven't much hope. How could I explain anything to you, compared with whom I am but a babbling babe?

Don't, don't talk like that. You'd do me a favor if you'd be a little more manly, more self-assured. What am I to do with a mere shadow of a guest? I'll blow him through the porthole into the lake. I need several explanations. You who roam around outside can give me them. But if you sit trembling at my table here and by self-deception forget the little you know, then you may as well clear out at once. What I mean, I say.

There's something in that. In fact, I am superior to you in some ways. So I'll try to control myself. Ask away!

Better, far better that you exaggerate in this direction and that you fancy yourself to be somehow superior. But you must understand me properly. I am a human being like you, I'm as many centuries more impatient as I am older than you. Well, let's talk about the masters. Listen! And drink some wine, to sharpen your wits. Don't be shy. Take a good swig. There's another large shipload there.

Gracchus, that's an excellent wine. Long live the master!

Pity that he died today. He was a good man

and he went peacefully. Healthy, grown-up children stood at his deathbed, his wife had fainted at the foot, but his last thought was for me. A good man, a Hamburger.

Heavens above, a Hamburger! And you down here in the south know that he died today?

What? I not know when my master dies? You're really a bit simple-minded.

Are you trying to insult me?

Not at all, I do it without meaning to. But you shouldn't be so surprised. Drink more wine. As for the masters, it's like this: Originally, the bark belonged to no one.

Gracchus, one request. First, tell me briefly but coherently how things are with you. To be truthful: I really don't know. You of course take these things for granted and assume, as is your way, that the whole world knows about them. But in this brief human life—and life really is brief, Gracchus, try to grasp that— in this brief life it's as much as one can do to get oneself and one's family through. Interesting as the Hunter Gracchus is—this is conviction, not flattery—there's no time to think of

him, to find out about him, let alone worry
about him. Perhaps on one's deathbed, like
your Hamburger, this I don't know. Perhaps
the busy man will then have a chance to stretch
out for the first time and let the green Hunter
Gracchus pass for once through his idle
thoughts. But otherwise, it's as I've said: I
knew nothing about you, business brought me
down here to the harbor, I saw the bark, the
gangplank lay ready, I walked across—but
now I'd like to know something coherent about
you.

Ah, coherent. That old, old story. All the
books are full of it, teachers draw it on the
blackboard in every school, the mother dreams
of it while suckling her child, lovers murmur
it while embracing, merchants tell it to the
customers, the customers to the merchants,
soldiers sing it on the march, preachers de-
claim it in church, historians in their studies
realize with open mouths what happened long
ago and never cease describing it, it is printed
in the newspapers and people pass it from hand
to hand, the telegraph was invented so that it
might encircle the world the faster, it is ex-

cavated from ruined cities and the elevator rushes it up to the top of the skyscraper. Railway passengers announce it from the windows to the countries they are passing through, but even before that the savages have howled it at them, it can be read in the stars and the lakes reflect it, the streams bring it down from the mountains and the snow scatters it again on the summit, and you, man, sit here and ask me for coherence. You must have had an exceptionally dissipated youth.

Possibly, as is typical of any youth. But it would be very useful, I think, if you would go and have a good look round the world. Strange as it may seem to you, and sitting here it surprises even me, it's a fact that you are not the talk of the town, however many subjects may be discussed you are not among them, the world goes its way and you go on your journey, but until today I have never noticed that your paths have crossed.

These are your observations, my dear friend, other people have made others. There are only two possibilities here. Either you conceal what you know about me, and do so with a definite motive. In which case let me tell you frankly: you are on the wrong track. Or you actually think that you can't remember me, because you confuse my story with someone else's. In that case I can only tell you: I am—no, I can't, everyone knows it and of all people I should be the one to tell you! It's so long ago. Ask the historians! Go to them, and then come back. It's so long ago. How can I be expected to keep it in this overcrowded brain?

Wait, Gracchus, I'll make it easier for you, I'll ask you some questions. Where do you come from?

From the Black Forest, as everyone knows.

From the Black Forest, of course. And was it there, round about the fourth century, that you used to hunt?

Man alive, do you know the Black Forest? No.

You really don't know anything. The helmsman's little child knows more than you, probably far more. Who on earth sent you in here? It's fate. Your obtrusive modesty was indeed only too well justified. You are a nonentity whom I'm filling up with wine. Now you don't even know the Black Forest. And I was born there. I hunted there until I was twenty-five. If only the chamois had not led me astray— well, now you know it—I'd have had a long pleasant hunter's life, but the chamois led me on, I fell down a precipice and was killed on the rocks. Don't ask any more. Here I am, dead, dead, dead. Don't know why I'm here. Was loaded onto the death-ship, as befits a miserable dead man, the three or four ministrations were performed upon me, as on everyone, why should they make an exception of the Hunter Gracchus? Everything was in order, I lay stretched out in the boat.

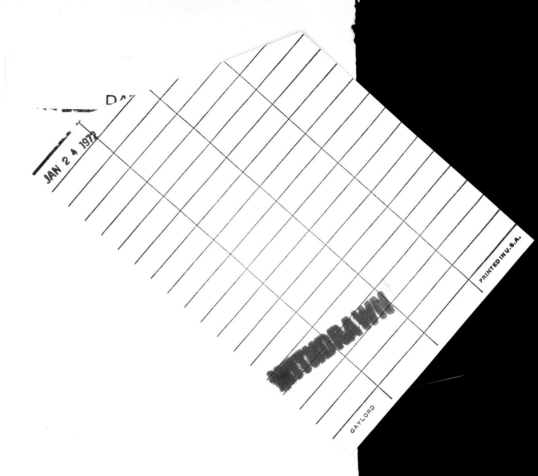